HOOPERMAN

ALSO BY JOHN M. DANIEL

Mysteries
Play Melancholy Baby
The Poet's Funeral
Vanity Fire
Behind the Redwood Door

Short Story Collections
The Woman by the Bridge
Generous Helpings

Cat Books
The Love Story of Sushi and Sashimi
The Ballad of Toby and Lark

Nonfiction
One for the Books
Structure, Style and Truth: Elements of the Short Story

Ebooks
Swimming in the Deep End
Geronimo's Skull
Elephant Lake
Promises, Promises, Promises

HOOPERMAN

a bookstore mystery

by

John M. Daniel

Oak Tree Press Hanford, CA

Oak Tree Press
Publishers Since 1998

First Edition, November 2013

ISBN 978-1-61009-061-2
LCCN 2012955894

Cover art:
"The Librarian," by André Martins de Barros, French painter based in Paris.
Copyright by the artist and protected by international copyright law.

for booksellers and former booksellers,

including, and especially,

Susan Daniel

HOOPERMAN

MAXWELL'S BOOKS STAFF

STORE OFFICE

Elmer Maxwell, Founder, Owner, and Manager
Bernice Rostov, Bookkeeper, Office Manager
Harry Thornton, Buyer

ON THE FLOOR
clerks and the sections they maintain

Jack Davis, Political Science, History
Pete Blanchard, Political Science, Biography
Bill Harper, Sports, Humor, Puzzles & Games, Reference
Lucinda Baylor, Cookbooks, Children's, Gardening, Eastern Thought
Tomás Cervantes, Sociology, The Times They Are A-Changin', Black Studies
Millie Larkin, Fiction, Literature, Genre Fiction, Best Sellers, Front Window
Peggy Chao, Women's, Gay, Human Sexuality, Health, Sports
Charles David, Art & Architecture, Photography
Jeanne McBurney, Religion, Reference, Pets
Abe Roth, Music, Humor, Travel

OTHERS

Martin West, Shipping and Receiving
Francis "Hoop" Johnson, Surveillance and Poetry
Howard Katz, Pest Control and Morale

CHAPTER ONE

Hooperman Johnson, a tall, skinny, bushy-bearded man of few words, lived that spring and summer of 1972 in a rented room with a bed, a chair, a table, and no phone over the 'At's Amore Pizza Palace on University Avenue in Palo Alto, California. It was convenient. Hoop worked downstairs as a pizza cook, earning minimum wage and all the pizza he could eat, which got to be less and less as time went by.

So on Monday, July 10, three months into the job, he wrote a letter of resignation on an 'At's Amore napkin, put it in his pocket, and walked across the street to Maxwell's Books. He'd been eyeing the sign in the window for two days: HELP WANTED. They knew him at Maxwell's. He was there every afternoon, usually straightening and reading his way through the poetry section. He even bought the occasional book.

"Hey, it's Hooperman!" Lucinda said from the bull pen, a

corral of counters where the staff could handle the register, greet customers, talk on the phone, and gossip with each other. Lucinda Baylor was a substantial brown woman with a generous smile and a topiary black hairdo. Like Hoop, she was about thirty years old. She was as tall as Hoop if you counted her Afro, and unlike Hoop, she was hefty. Not fat, *zaftig*. Tall and pillowy. "Haven't seen you here since yester-day," she said.

"The deh,deh,day's young yet," Hoop said. "How you dud, how you dud, how you duh,duh,dud...oing, Luce?"

"Day's young yet. So far so good. You?"

"That sign in the window. You guh,guh,guh,guys guh,got a juh,dge...ob for sale?"

Lucinda shook her head. "Yes, but you wouldn't want it."

"Are you ki,ki,ki,kidding?"

"Not this job."

"Who do I tuh,tuh,tut...alk—"

"Elmer," she said. "He's in his office. But really, Hoop, you're not the type."

"What does it teh,teh,teh,take to sell bub...bub...bub...b—"

Lucinda rolled her eyes heavenward. "Elmer doesn't want a clerk, Hoop. Elmer wants to hire a cop. A pig."

Hooperman grinned and said, on the first try, "Oink."

He walked back through the labyrinth of aisles to the office, halfway to the back of the store. He knocked, then pushed the door open. A gray-haired woman and a middle-aged man looked up from their desks. The woman said, "Yes?"

"I'm here to see Elmer," Hoop said.

The man pointed over his shoulder with his thumb. "Inner sanctum," he said.

"Thanks." Hoop walked into the office inside the office. Elmer Maxwell looked up from his desk, pulled his reading glasses down on his nose, and looked over the top. He told Hoop he was busy, but the words he used were, "Can I help you?"

Elmer Maxwell was famous, at least in Palo Alto, as a bookseller; and beyond Palo Alto he was famous as a fierce pacifist. He had refused to serve in World War II, choosing Civilian Public Service instead. He had protested Korea before protesting was fashionable, he had marched against the Vietnam War alongside Dr. King and Joan Baez, and his store had been fire bombed twice. Earlier that year, 1972, Elmer's face had glowered from the cover of *Time*. He was a grizzly-bearded, handsome bear in a frayed tweed coat.

Hoop scratched his own beard and took a deep breath. "It's about the juh,dge job. That sss...hign in the window."

Elmer smiled kindly and said, "I don't think you're right for the job, my friend."

"Why?"

"You're the man they call Hooperman, right? The pizza delivery guy? But you're famous. My staff loves you!"

"Chef, actually. Name's Hoop. Hoop Juh,dge...ohnson. Hooperman's a ni,ni,ninnnickname."

"How'd you get that name, anyway? Hoop? Tall guy like you, I bet you played basketball in high school. Am I right?"

"Not even cuh,cuh,close."

"Whatever. The point is—"

"I'm not a delivery guh,guh,guy. I only deliver to this ssst, to here. I love this sss...tore. About the juh,dge...ob—"

"Hoop, please sit down."

Hoop sat.

Elmer folded his hands on the desk and gave Hoop the famous kind, black-eyed glare. "This is not the job for you. Trust me."

"Howk, howkuh,kuh,come?"

Elmer paused, then asked, "Hooperman, do you know what shrinkage is?"

Hoop shook his head.

"Let me give you a basic lesson in economics. I have inventory, the rest of the world has money. I give them some inventory, they give me some money. You with me so far?"

Hoop nodded.

Elmer Maxwell's eyebrows formed a battle line. "If I have a hundred dollars worth of books, and over the course of a year I take in ten bucks in exchange for books, I should have ninety dollars worth of books left on my shelves, right?"

"Meh,meh,makes ss,hense."

"Right. Makes sense. So you tell me why in June of this year I closed the store to do our annual physical inventory, and when the numbers came to rest, I was nineteen thousand dollars in the hole. *In the hole.*"

The Elmer Maxwell now standing up behind his desk was not the cranky businessman too busy to talk to Hoop when he first walked into the office. Nor was he the affable celebrity who had called Hoop famous. This Elmer was a tall, balding, furious victim who had been robbed—*robbed*—out of nineteen thousand dollars.

"It may be one bastard, or it may be a gang of bastards, or it may be a whole ill-mannered generation of bastards, but I'm going to stop them," he said. "And you, Hoop Johnson, are not the man to do it."

"Howk, howk—"

"Oh, stop it. Please. Unless I'm mistaken, you have difficulty expressing yourself, right?"

"Only when I speh,ssspeh,speh,sss...peak."

Elmer shrugged. "Well, this is a speaking role, my friend."

"Only a pup...roblem with cuh,cuh,consonants. Only some. Okay with vowels. Muh,muh,mostly. Teh,tell me about the juh,dge...ob."

Another shrug. Another sigh. "I'm looking for a sneak to prowl the aisles of my store for hours, pretending to browse the books."

"I'm into that," Hoop said. "For sure."

"Wait. You're not really browsing. That's one of the reasons you're not right for the job. You'll spend your energy looking at the books, not the bastards."

"Any other reasons?"

"Yes. Okay, so you spot a man stuffing a book into the back of his pants, then letting his shirt drop down and cover the evidence. He walks out of the store. Are you up to following this thief out of the store and stopping him on University Avenue and saying, 'Excuse me, sir, I want you to show me what you have stuffed in the back of your pants?'"

Hoop thought about it. Stupid job. Then he thought about being able to browse the shelves of Maxwell's Books—for pay.

"I'm your muh,muh,muh,mmm...an."

"You think you'll be able to argue with some hard-headed fast-talker?" Elmer asked.

"I'm duh,duh,doing that right now."

Elmer laughed all the air out of his barrel chest and shook his head. "Well, kiddo, nobody else wants the job. So we'll go with the Hooperman."

Hoop grinned.

"I'm not putting you on payroll."

"What do you meh,meh,mean?"

"You're not a member of the staff, understand? No health shit. No workman's comp, disability, all that."

"I already have a di,di,di,disability."

"I'm paying you under the table, five dollars a day in cash, seven days a week, plus half—that's fifty percent—of whatever you save me by busting those assholes who are robbing me blind. I call that fair. You?"

"Fair. Where do I ss...ign?"

Elmer sighed. "You don't sign. This is under the table. You haven't listened to a word I've said, have you?"

Back in the front of the store, Howard Katz, another member of the Maxwell's Books family, was sitting on the front counter and Lucinda was scratching him behind the ears. Hoop told her he had taken the job and she looked at him with sad eyes.

"Now who's going to bring us pizza?" she asked. She placed a hand on his cheek.

Hoop rubbed his hand over Howard's handsome face and head and Howard stood up, turned around, lifted his tail, showed off his butt, then settled down again in front of Lucinda.

"I'll feh,feh,feh,fetch the pih,pizza for you, same as always," Hoop said. "But from now on I'll guh,guh,guh,go as an errand boy, not a chef."

"Aw jeez, Hoop." She stabbed her hair with a pencil and shook her head.

Hoop grinned. "I consider it a puh,puh,pro...muh,motion!"

He took the 'At's Amore paper napkin out of his shirt pocket, kissed it, and carried it across the street to his former boss. *Arrivederci, Roma.*

Hoop started the next morning, when the store opened at ten. By one o'clock he had the whole poetry section dusted, tidied up, and re-alphabetized, with his favorite poets faced out on the shelves. Matthew Arnold. J. V. Cunningham. Emily Dickinson. Jane Gillis. *Jane Gillis.* He faced out each of her three titles. Susan MacDonald. Rob Swigart. Al Young....

"Hey, man."

He looked up from the bottom shelf he was giving a last touch to and saw Abe Roth smiling down at him. Abe was a guitarist who performed around town, mostly at a coffee house called Saint Michael's Alley. In the daytime he clerked at Maxwell's Books, where he took care of the music section. He was a stocky man with a pearly smile that glowed out from a black forest of beard.

Hoop stood up and said, "Hello, Abe."

"You don't know me," Abe reminded him. "We were all briefed this morning. We don't know you, and you don't know us, according to Elmer."

"Right. Ss...horry, whoever you are."

"Speaking of Elmer, he told me to send you back to his office."

"Uh-oh."

"Yeah, he's got a bug up his ass." Abe smiled and shrugged. "As usual."

Hoop sauntered back to the office and walked into Elmer's inner sanctum.

Elmer looked up from his desk and said, "Hoop Johnson, how many rip-off artists have you caught so far?"

"Uh—"

"You think I don't have eyes?" he demanded. He stood up. "Huh? Just because I'm back here in this office doesn't mean I don't know what's going on out on the floor. You've spent three hours in the God damned poetry section. How many people rip off poetry books, do you know?"

Hoop said, "None so fah,fah,far today."

"None so far this year. And you know why?"

"Um—"

"Because nobody goes in the God damned poetry section. Now get out there and prowl the aisles where people are stealing books."

"Any hints?" Hoop asked.

Elmer sat down and slumped back in his chair. He shook his head and gave Hoop a wise, sad smile. "I'm sorry to have to say this, my friend, but the worst offenders are the reformers, the radicals, the pacifists and scofflaws I most admire. They steal political science books, left-wing shit. The hippies and the yippies. They wear a peace sign or a Mao badge or a Che Guevara tee shirt and they think that entitles them to steal from the only store that's brave enough to sell their kind of books. Well, fuck 'em. They may want to fix the world, but as far as I'm concerned, they're thieves. Go out there and bust their asses. Oh, yeah. Keep an eye on the drug section, too."

"Okuh,kay." Hoop had finished up in the poetry section anyway.

"And another thing."

"Mm?"

Elmer fished his wallet out of a back pocket and pulled out a ten. "Go across the street and get me a medium sausage and onion. Put some red pepper flakes on it."

Maxwell's Books was a temple, a palace, an architectural wonder: a vast cavern with cement and linoleum floors, chipped plaster walls, and skylights of frosted glass reinforced by chicken wire, a converted warehouse filled with a labyrinth of crude pine bookshelves. A place to get lost among miles of books. A drafty space in winter, a cooker in summer, it smelled of tobacco, dust, a hint of mildew, and mostly books.

Hoop loved that smell.

Even so, he thought his first day on the job would never end. After Elmer Maxwell reminded him he wasn't there for his own enjoyment, he settled down and lurked around aisle after aisle, pretending not to be at all interested in what his fellow browsers were up to. He recognized most of them from the many hours he had spent browsing in the same aisles with them over the months: bearded freaks and suits on lunch break, women in jeans with babies strapped to their backs, tweedy types from the Stanford faculty, teenagers with long and greasy hair. This was the first time it had ever occurred to Hoop to pay them any attention, let alone suspicion. It appeared they were up to nothing more than browsing. Now and then they'd find something worth keeping, but instead of concealing it and sneaking out, they'd carry the book or books up to the check-out area in the front, where Charley David and Millie Larkin were stationed at the cash registers.

As far as Hoop could tell, nobody was robbing Elmer Maxwell blind, which was lucky for Elmer and lucky for Hoop, but not very satisfying for either one of them. He moseyed slowly through Political Science, Sociology, Religion, Eastern Thought, Women's Studies, Arts & Crafts, The Times They Are A-Changin', Biography, Black Studies, History, Art & Architecture, Music, Gardening, Cookbooks, Pets, Human Sexuality, Games & Puzzles, Reference, Travel, Kids Books, Sports, Humor, and on into the enormous back room just for fiction, and then back once again to The Times They Are A-Changin', where Elmer had predicted he would find people ready to take Abbie Hoffman's advice and *Steal This Book*.

No luck, and by five o'clock Hooperman was feeling tired and worthless. He walked into the staff kitchen and put his hand on the side of the coffee urn. Hot. He pulled a mug from the shelf, and while he was drawing a half-cup of joe, he heard, "So Hooper. How's it going, babe?"

He turned around and found Lucinda Baylor grinning. She wore a tie-dyed tee shirt too small for all of her and a pair of short, frayed cut-offs.

"Hi, Luce," he said. He sighed and shook his head.

"Looks to me as if somebody needs a hug."

"Who mi,mi,me?"

She grinned. "That makes two of us. C'mere."

She not only hugged him, she squeezed his buns a bit, and yes, he squeezed hers back. Well, why not?

"Nice," she murmured. "You're divorced, right? That's what I heard."

"Yah."

"Awww."

"Nah," Hoop said. "I'm beh,beh,beb...etter off."

"Tell me about it." Then she laughed and added, "I don't mean that literally, of course. I just mean I hear you." She went to the wall above the counter where each member of the staff—including Howard Katz—had a cubbyhole. She rifled through whatever she kept in her cubby, removed a small piece of paper, folded it twice, and pushed it into the front pocket of her cut-offs. Smiled.

"Hey, buh,buh,by the way, Lucinda, what ss...hections do you teh,take care of?"

"Cookbooks, Children's, Gardening, Eastern Thought."

"Much shhh...rinkage in your ss—?"

"Nobody steals Cookbooks, Children's Books, or Gardening. Eastern Thought, all the time. Especially yoga and shit. It's like we're just giving away *Be Here Now*." She patted Hoop's cheek and said, "Later, sweet thing," then left the kitchen, gently patting her buns as she walked through the door.

He reported to Elmer at the end of the day. "I preveh,veh,vented some pih,pih,people from shoplifting. Kid buh,buh,brrrousing *The Sensuous Woman*. Suspuh,spicious. He saw me stut,aring at him and puh,put it bubbubb...away. Mi,moved on."

"You didn't catch him in the act, though," Elmer pointed

out.

"I saved you some muh,muh,muh,mmm...money."

"And now this kid knows not to steal my books while you're watching him. Great."

Hoop hung his head. "Mmmaybe I'm not cuh,cuh,cut out for this jud,dge...ob."

"I told you that yesterday, kiddo."

Hoop nodded.

Elmer smiled. "Hoop, I want you to stay on. Nobody hits a homer first time at bat." He reached into a drawer and pulled out a five, which he handed across the desk.

"Guh,good," Hoop said. "Because I buh,buh,burned my bub...ridges at the pip,pip,pip... 'At's Amuh,more."

"But my God, man, how will you survive on five bucks a day?"

"Muh,maybe I'll get lucky, cuh,cuh,catch somebody."

On his way to the front of the store, Hoop walked through the poetry aisle one more time, just to see if all was as he'd left it. There, slouching with his back against Essays, was a lanky young man with a wispy blond goatee. He wore a rumpled lightweight sport coat, and he was fingering his way through a hardback book. He put the book back on the shelf, down among the Rs, then took out the book next to it, casually slipped it under his arm, *under his coat,* and walked out of the poetry section, toward the front of the store.

Hoop checked. Missing book. He knew which one.

He followed the young man to the front of the store, nodding at Millie as he tailed the suspect right past the register and out onto University Avenue. He followed the non-paying customer around the corner to the Maxwell's parking lot behind the store. Just as the young man was opening the door of his green Chevy Nova, Hoop said, "Hey."

The man frowned at him. "Yes?"

"Adrienne Rich," Hoop said. "You like her?"

The man nodded. "I collect her. First editions. Are you a fan of hers?"

"You beh,beh,beh,beb...et. What's your nname?"

"Lawrence Holgerson," he said. He held out his hand. "And yours?"

"Cuh,cuh,could I see your receipt for that buh, buh, bub... ook?"

"Who are you, anyway?"

"Fellow feh,feh,fan." Hoop held out his hand, but not for a handshake. "The receipt. Or the buh,book."

"You've got a lot of nerve." Lawrence Holgerson's voice was trembling. His goatee was trembling, too.

Hoop's outstretched hand felt like trembling too, but he didn't let it show. "Gi,gi,gi,give me."

Holgerson shook his head, a definite no. "Fuck you, Porky Pig."

Hoop walked around to the back of the Nova and read the license plate aloud, twice. No stammer. No problem reading aloud. Loud and clear.

"Fuck you," Lawrence Holgerson repeated. He pulled the book from under his armpit and handed it to Hoop. Adrienne Rich, *The Will to Change,* first edition. "See if I ever shop in this store again." He climbed into his car and slammed the door. He lit a cigarette and cranked on the ignition, then sped out of the parking lot.

Hoop sauntered back to the front of the store, grinned at Millie and Charley, and marched back to Elmer's office. He walked in and plopped the book on the boss's desk.

Elmer picked it up and asked, "What's this?"

And Hooperman bowed and said, suave and unfaltering as Cary Grant, "I caught a thief."

HOW HOOPERMAN
GOT HIS NAME

When Frankie Johnson was four years old, he took a safety pin from his mother's sewing basket and pinned the end of a red towel around his neck, so that the towel hung down his back like a cape. Grinning, he paraded into the kitchen and said, "Mum mum Mommy."

Clara turned from the sink and returned his grin.

"Hi, Frankie," she said.

"I'm Hooperman!" he announced.

"Why so you are! That's wonderful, sweetheart!"

Frankie shook his head, still grinning. "Nnn,duh,don't cuh,cuh,call me Wheetheart, cuc,call me Hooperman!"

"Okay, Superman!" his mother said. She sat on the kitchen stool and held out her arms. "Will you still be my sweetheart, Superman?"

"Later!"

Frankie burst out the kitchen screen door and ran to the

playground in the center of the apartment complex. "Hey!"
he shouted to a dozen kids on swings and on the slide and in
the sandbox and running around the lawn. "Hey! Look at
mi,mi,mi,mmee! I'm Hooooperman!"

Five minutes later, when he shambled back through the
kitchen door, he climbed onto his mother's lap. She was still
sitting on the stool. He snuffled, and she dried his tears, hid-
ing her own.
"Juh,dge...immy..."
"Jimmy O'Brien?"
"All of them! They muh,muh,meh,meh,make fuff... fuff...
ff—!"
"I know, sweetheart. I know."
He howled and squirmed.
"I know, Superman. I know it's hard."

CHAPTER TWO

Hooperman worked at the store almost a week before he caught another shoplifter, a teenager who had stuffed a *Zap Comix* under his Steely Dan concert tee shirt. The comic book was priced at half a dollar, so Hoop earned an extra twenty-five cents that day. Elmer was good about paying him his five dollars a day, and Hoop was still having a good time, so he decided to continue working at Maxwell's Books as long as he could afford it.

It was easy work, although it was boring as dust except when he played like a customer and actually got interested in the books he was guarding. Howard Katz sometimes kept him company, following him around and hitting him up for attention. Hoop made friends with more of the staff, including a couple of Elmer's old conscientious objector cronies from WWII, Pete Blanchard and Jack Davis, who squabbled over the right to take care of the Political Science section. Pete was a socialist, Jack was an anarchist, and their arguments stopped traffic all over the store. Neither one of them wanted anything to do with the section that Charley David had named The Times They Are A-Changin'. Kids' stuff, they called it. Kids don't know shit, they said. Charley was a painter whose jeans looked like a used palette.

"Kids these days," Pete muttered one day when he and Jack were elbowing each other in the Politics aisle. Hooperman stood by, supposedly doing his job, mainly eavesdropping. Pete wore a jacket and tie to work and looked like a rumpled professor.

"Aaaah, give it a rest," Jack countered. "You political dinosaur." He hitched up his overalls and lit a Lucky Strike.

"No smoking in the store."

"Says who?"

"Can't you see this place is a tinderbox, Jack? You want to burn the store down?"

Jack turned to Hoop, raised his eyebrows, wiggled his cigarette, and said, "Now there's an idea."

Friday afternoon Hoop stopped by the front counter to see how Lucinda was doing. She and Millie Larkin, who tended the fiction section when she wasn't punching the cash register, were out of the bull pen, rearranging the front window display to accommodate a STOP THE WAR banner Charley had made.

"Lookin' guh,guh,gug...ood, ladies," Hoop said.

Millie gave Hoop a look that warned him never to call her a lady again. She was a small, wiry woman whose closest approximation of a friendly smile was to slightly relax her glare.

Lucinda smiled and said, "Hoop, dollbaby, would you go see if Martin will let us have a couple of his precious boxes? We need to store some stock under the counter."

"Who's Mah,mah,mah,Martin?" Hoop asked.

Millie said, "You haven't met Martin yet?" She chuckled.
"Good luck."

"Back of the store," Lucinda said. "The back room? Shipping and Receiving? Door says 'Staff only'?"

"Don't get him started," Millie cautioned. "Martin, I mean."

"Mah,mah,Martin's—"

"Martin's a sweetheart," Lucinda assured Hoop. "Really."

Millie added, "Keep reminding yourself of that. And don't get him started. Don't let him give you any shit."

"What kind?" Lucinda said, and they both cracked up.

Hoop knocked.

No answer.

He opened the door and walked into the Shipping and Receiving department, where he saw rough pine shelves loaded with tidy bundles of assorted books and a long Masonite counter neatly arranged with piles of new titles. The far wall was occupied by a thrift-store desk and a dented green filing cabinet. The floor was arranged in rows and columns of unopened cartons, and empty cartons were nested and stacked to the ceiling against the far wall. The room was lit by a flickering fluorescent ceiling fixture and one open window, which allowed a spotlight of sunbeam to shine through a ballet of dust motes.

Then the hulk standing at the counter turned to face Hoop, a twitching snarl on his kisser. He nodded his head, then shook it. "What the horseshit do you want?" he asked. "Can't you read, in the horseshit pigshit? Staff only."

Martin looked about fifty. He was a few inches taller than Hoop, he outweighed Hoop by at least fifty pounds, his head was shaved bald, his gray beard was a briar patch, he wore oily jeans and a gray tee shirt, and on his feet he wore dirt.

"Horseshit pigshit cowshit," he added through the snarl, and Hoop had a feeling there was a lot more Martin would have said if he weren't, in Lucinda's words, a sweetheart, really. He nodded, then shook his head again. His face was a dance of twitching creases.

Hoop tended to get politer than he felt, whenever he was confronted with a cross between a grizzly bear and a time bomb. He held out his hand and smiled. "Hoop Juh,juh,dge... ohnson. I'm new on the stuh,tuh,sst...aff."

Martin nodded and shook Hoop's hand. His grip was huge but gentle. "What do you want?"

Hoop realized at this point that the snarl was not going to go away. It was a permanent fixture, but it didn't mean much. "Muh,millie and Lucinda would like to have a cuh,cuh,couple of empty buh,buh,bub...cuh,cartons." He nodded at the wall of cardboard boxes built against the far wall. "For a puh,puh,project they're duh,duh,dud...fufffuff...the front window."

"Horseshit pigshit cowshit dogshit."

"Pah,pah,pah,pardon?"

The nod-shake again. Then he wiped the back of his hand across his snarl. "Can't have any of those," he said. "I'm saving those for returns. Returns? You got no idea. Horseshit."

"Um," Hoop said. "Only tum,tum...teh,teh,temporary."

"Out back," Martin said. "I threw a bunch of damaged boxes out there this morning, next to the damned Dumpster. Haven't broken them down yet. Gotta do that before the fire marshal has my ass. Horseshit pigshit."

"Out bub—?"

Nodded. "Through EMERGENCY EXIT ONLY."

"Alarm won't gug—"

"Busted." Martin's snarl gradually grew into a grin. "I busted it myself."

<<<>>>

It was hot out there in the parking lot, and the air next to the Dumpster stank. Not of trash or garbage, but of marijuana, which three Maxwell's Books clerks were sharing on a break. Hoop had to approach them to get to the cardboard boxes Martin had thrown away. Abe Roth, the guitarist who took care of the music section, grinned and announced, "It's the Hooperman!" He held the stubby brown joint out to the Hooperman, but the Hooperman declined with a wave of his hand.

"Smatter, Hoop?" Peggy Chao asked. "Still hooked on reality?"

"He needs a support group," Bill Harper said. "Like us."

The store's back door burst open and Elmer Maxwell charged out into the parking lot. He looked at the four of them and frowned. "What's going on here, people?"

Abe was the first to respond. "Uh, hey, Elmer. Like we were like having a you know, like, doob? Want a hit?"

"I most certainly do not. Why are the four of you out here when the store's full of customers? Huh?"

"Elmer, Elmer, calm down, man," Peggy said. "We're on a break, man."

"You're not going to bust us for doing a little herb?" Bill asked.

Elmer threw his hands in the air. "I couldn't care less what kind of stupid thing you want to do to yourself on your own time, people. But damn it, we've got a bookstore to run. Now get the hell in there and help customers. No, wait. Chew some gum or something first, for God's sake. And if I get any complaints from the customers, you're fired. Every fucking one of you. Okay?"

Peggy said, "Sheesh."

Abe grinned and bobbed his head. "Rat own, ma man."

The three dopin' clerks trucked on back into the grind, and Hoop turned to pick up cartons from the side of the dumpster.

"Hoop, you're the one I really wanted to talk to," Elmer said. "You're not loaded too, are you?"

"Nnnaw."

"Good. I need to talk to you. Come see me in my office." He turned and walked back into the store.

Hoop dropped the boxes off in the front of the store and Lucinda gave him a hug. Between Lucinda's hugs and Elmer's five bucks a day, Hoop felt like the best-paid bookstore cop in town.

Howard Katz crawled into one of the boxes.

When Hoop arrived in front of Elmer's desk, the boss looked up over his glasses and brought his eyebrows together. "Sit down," he said. Hoop took a chair opposite Elmer, who said, "Do you know the difference between outside shrinkage and inside shrinkage?"

Hoop shook his head. "Shush—"

"Shut up and listen, kiddo. Okay. Outside shrinkage, that's where the bastards come in off the street and rip me off."

"Sss...ho far, I haven't—"

"Lemme talk. Outside shrinkage isn't the killer. I'm more concerned about inside shrinkage. That's when you get ripped off by your loyal employees. Follow?"

"Pi,pi,pi,people who work here would sti,sti,ti,ti,steal bub-bub—?"

Elmer nodded with a fierce squint.

"But why? Staff get a di,di,discount."

Elmer shook his head sadly. "You're a babe in the woods, my friend. A lamb among the wolves. My staff is robbing me blind. Blind."

"Well, I—"

"So here's what we're going to do. What *you're* going to do. Keep on pretending to look for shoplifters. That's what the staff will think you're doing. Fine, let them think that, and if you catch somebody ripping off a book now and then, great. But the people I want you to really keep an eye on—and you have to keep this secret—are the staff. Make friends with them. Find out who's taking what books home at the end of the day. Make me a list."

You're a nutcase, Hoop thought. Out loud he said, "Guh,guh,gotcha."

"And another thing." Elmer took off his glasses, held them up to the light, blew dust off the lenses, and put them back on his nose. "You hear anybody badmouthing me, I want to know about it. I don't care what people think of me, that's their business. But if you hear somebody calling me an ass-hole, it's probably because they're looking for a justification, figure it's okay to rip off an asshole. So I need to know who's saying what."

A certified, paranoid nutcase. Nixon, for Christ's—

"Here's your five dollars for the day." Elmer pulled out his wallet and handed a fiver across the desk.

Hoop took the money, stood up, and decided to spend the rest of the afternoon straightening the poetry section. He fig-ured it was his last day working for Maxwell's Books, so he might as well enjoy it.

That evening, Hoop went over to 'At's Amore to buy a large salami, mushroom, onion, and olive, which he brought back to the evening shift, consisting of Millie in the back room tending to her fiction, and Charley and Lucinda taking turns on the register and shelving books in the front of the store.

And Hoop in the aisles, trawling for thieves. And Howard Katz, who swayed through the aisles dusting the bottom shelves with his tail. Hoop put the pizza on the counter in the staff kitchen. Charley had brought in a sixpack of Dos Equis.

It was a busy evening, following a fast day of crackling sales. Lucinda put KLOK-AM on the radio and piped oldies through the store. The staff took turns ducking back into the kitchen for a nosh on the fly. They knew what Friday evenings were like; a horde would swarm into the store when the Varsity Theater let out. "Play It Again, Sam" had been there for a month and was still drawing a crowd.

Hoop finished his pizza and beer and moseyed up to the register to see how things were going. Charley was straightening his art books, and Lucinda was between sales. She slipped Hoop a ten-dollar bill. "For the pizza. Delicious, as always."

"It's okay," Hoop said, sliding the bill back across the counter. "On mi,mim...me."

"Screw that." Lucinda winked. "On Elmer."

"Elmer know that?"

"He doesn't need to know that," she said. "We had a dynamite day, and besides, I didn't take a dinner hour. Elmer can really be a butt, you know?"

"Oh."

"What's the matter?"

Hoop shook his head. What the hell, he thought. It was his last day on the job. He thought of telling her that, but the words failed him.

"Hoop, would you do me a favor?"

Hoop nodded and smiled. "What's up?"

"Millie and Charley want to leave early tonight. Like ten? Together? So I was wondering if you'd hang around till closing. Thing is, I don't like being here on my own at night. All by myself. Would you—"

"Of cuh,cuh,cuh,cuh...course."

"And don't go wandering around in the back room, just stay up front, keep an eye on me?"

"My puh,puh,pleasure."

"My hero!" she said, lifting his knuckles to her lips.

God, she had pretty brown eyes.

Lucinda and Hoop shooed the last of the browsers out of the store at eleven, after she had rung up the last copy from what had been a foot-high stack of *I'm OK—You're OK*. She locked the front door and Hoop went back through the store to make sure nobody was left inside. He turned off the light in the kitchen, where Howard was asleep in his cubby. The light in Shipping and Receiving was already off, and the office door was locked.

The coast was clear.

Hoop reached the front counter just as Lucinda finished counting the till and running the register tape. "How'd we duh,duh,do?"

"Whoa!" She ran her fingers down the register tape and grinned. "Fourteen hundred and eighty-two dollars and forty-seven cents! That's the biggest day since Christmas!" She stuffed a wad of cash and checks into a small paper bag, folded it up, and sealed it with Scotch tape. "We leave nineteen dollars and seventy-two cents in the register," she told him. "Easy number to remember, right? And we leave the cash drawer open, so if anybody breaks into the store they don't destroy the register."

"What do you duh,duh,do with that sack? That's a lot of muh,money."

"We hide it. Want to know where?"

"No."

"Then go get lost for a few minutes. I'll take care of this. I go put it behind some books, then I leave a note in Bernice's cubby in the kitchen, with the section, author, and title where the treasure's buried."

Hoop nodded. "You tut,ake cuh,cuh...care of that, and I'll guh,guh,go around the store one more tuh,tuh,tuh,tuh—"

"Cool. Hey, pick me up a copy of Erica Jong's *Fruits and Vegetables*. I want to borrow it."

"Is that allowed?" Hoop asked.

"Who's to know?" she answered.

Out on University Avenue, in the hot June evening, they stood in front of the Maxwell's Books window admiring the STOP THE WAR sign and the lit-up display of current best-sellers. The store behind the display was dark and the doors were locked.

Lucinda stuffed the front door key into her jeans pocket. "So," she said, her index finger pulling on the neck of her tee shirt. "You live over there, huh? Above the pizza parlor?"

"Yep. I duh,duh,duh,dream of peh,pepperoni a lot. So your cuh,cuh,cuh,car's in the lot behind the ss...tore?"

She pulled him into her arms. "Yep," she whispered.

Hoop trembled in her embrace and held his breath, then took a deep whiff of her afro and let it out. "Shall I walk you to your cuh,cuh,car?" he squeaked.

She murmured, "Your apartment is closer."

HOW HOOPERMAN
LEARNED TO SING

One of the happiest moments of Clara Johnson's life was the evening her son, Frankie, aged five, grinned and nodded when she asked the musical question, "Next time won't you sing with me?"

He did. They sang together, and she was astounded. Carefully, she said, "Lovely. Just lovely. Now can you sing it by yourself?"

"A-B-C-D-E-F-G," he chanted. He stood up on the bed and continued, "H-I-J-K-LMNO-P!"

He jumped up and down, landed on his butt and laughed out loud. "Q-R-S, T-U-V, W-X, Y and Z...."

He bounced from the bed and into her open arms. "Now I know my A-B-C's! Muh,muh,Mom, I know my A Buh,buh,B Sss...C's!"

"You sure do, my darling," she answered, wiping tears from her eyes. "I'm so proud of you!"

"You know what?"

"What, sweetheart?"

"That su...hong sss...hounds like Buh,buh,Bah, Bah—"

"'Baa Baa Black Sheep'? I know! And what else? Another song, too!"

He thought hard, then nodded. "Tuh,tut...Winkle Winkle!"

"That's right, honey! Will you sing that one for me?"

Frankie walked to the center of his room, hiked up his pajama bottoms, bowed, and sang, in the sweetest monotone his mother had ever heard, "Twinkle twinkle little star, how I wonder what you are. Up above the world so high, like a diamond in the sky, twinkle, twinkle, little star. How I wonder what you are." When he finished, he grinned again, and bowed again.

Clara clapped her hands. "Darling, you can sing!"

He couldn't, really. The child couldn't carry a tune. But he could carry the words!

CHAPTER THREE

When Hooperman opened his apartment door for her, she asked, "What? You don't lock?"

"Why buh,buh,buh,bother?" he asked.

"You're too sweet for your own good."

Hoop lit the pole lamp and showed her his home: one room with a kitchen area (hot plate, sink, half-fridge, cupboard, and counter) on one side, the rest filled with thrift store furniture: a Formica-topped kitchen table and four chairs, a double bed and end table, a dresser, a brick-and-board bookcase, and an overstuffed armchair. He pointed to the two doors on the other side of the bed. "Cuh,cuh,closet, buh,bathroom."

"Nice," Lucinda said. She set the copy of *Fruits and Vegetables* on the kitchen table, walked to his bookcase, and ran a finger over the spines. "You have all three of Jane Gillis's books," she noticed. "In hardback. You must like her."

Hoop didn't answer.

She pulled a volume out and opened it. "Signed! 'To Francis, with love. Janie.' Janie? Francis? Who's Francis?"

"Mi,mi,mim...I am."

"You know Jane Gillis? *The* Jane Gillis? She's just *Janie* to you?"

Hoop didn't answer.

Lucinda walked to the window and looked down on the lights of University Avenue. "That's our store." She pulled the shade down and turned. "Uh...."

Hoop crossed the room to her, put his hands on her hips, and looked into her kind eyes. "Yes?"

"I'm a little nervous," she said. "First-time jitters. You know."

"Want to smoke a juh,dge...oint? That help?"

Lucinda shuddered. "I never smoke that stuff. Does bad things to me. Talk about nervous."

"Mi,mi,mim... Well—"

"Besides, it gives me the munchies, and that's one thing I do not need, thank you very much indeed, and, oh God... Hoop, could we like turn off that light? I'm kind of shy. I mean, we're going to do our thing, right?"

"I sure hope so."

"Thing is, I'm like I said, shy. Because I'm what you might call...heavy?"

Hoop went to the pole lamp and turned it off. "Ceh,ceh,ceh,candle?" he asked the silhouette against the window shade.

"Oh. Yeah, that would be far out, I guess." Without much conviction.

"I duh,don't have a ceh,ceh,candle."

She laughed out loud across the dark. "C'mere, you."

By the time Hoop reached her, she was completely out of her clothes. She didn't feel heavy. Unless you mean like a rich dessert.

"I'm a little shy muh,muh,myself," he said. "It's bib...een so long..."

"Tell me about it. I haven't had any for weeks."

"Muh,muh,muh,months," he said. Years, really, but he didn't want to sound desperate.

"We better do something about that, my man." She worked on the shirt buttons while he dealt with the belt buckle and slipped out of his sandals. When their clothes lay in a mixed jumble on the linoleum, they baby-stepped to the bed, where she toppled him down onto his back and climbed in after him, her soft laugh light with pleasure, the scent of her body heavy with desire.

"Who needs a ceh,ceh,candle?" said Hooperman.

"I'm just happy you can't see me."

"But I ceh,can."

"Believe me, baby, by tomorrow—"

"Believe me," Hoop said, "if all those endearing young charms, which I gaze on so fondly today, were to change by tomorrow, and fleet in my arms, like fairy-gifts fading away, thou wouldst still be adored, as this moment thou art, let thy loveliness fade as it will, and around the dear ruin each wish of my heart would entwine itself verdantly still."

"Holy shit."

"Holy shu,shush...what?"

"You can talk! Now shut up and kiss me."

It was a short night of heavy slumber and sweet awakenings. But at about four, Hoop woke up and found nobody beside him. Lucinda's scent still filled the bed, and her spot was warm and damp with sweat, but it was empty.

Then the toilet flushed and she came out of the bathroom. Good. No, not good. She was dressed.

"You're leaving?"

"Gotta go, sweet thing," she answered. She bent down and kissed his lips.

"Buh,buh—"

"I left my purse in the store. Gotta get it, then run home and take care of some stuff. See you Monday? Afternoon shift?"

"Well, uh, how abuh,buh,bout Ss...aturday evening? Sunday buh,breakfast? What abuh,bout—"

The world blew apart.

The noise shattered the night, rattled the building, and echoed in the empty street. Hoop leapt out of bed and they ran together to the window. She jerked on the string and the window shade whizzed up into the roller and went *thup-thup-thup*. They looked down on a disaster across the street. The plate glass was smashed to smithereens, the spotlight aimed at the display had been blown out, and the books in the window were on fire.

"That's our store!" Lucinda said for the second time that night. She gasped. "Hoop, call 9-1-1!"

"No tuh,tut...elephone."

"Oh dear Lord. I have to get down there!"

"Hold on," Hoop said. "Let me get duh,duh,dressed."

But she didn't wait. By the time Hoop reached the street she had unlocked the front door of the store, and by the time he got across the street she had disappeared into the smoky building, leaving the door wide open behind her. From what he could see the fire hadn't gone beyond the window display, but the smoke and stench were sickening. All those books!

A chorus of sirens grew louder and louder, coming from both directions. Before Hoop could follow Lucinda into the store, a black-and-white pulled up beside the curb, flashing a blue and red light show on the wall of the building, the siren dying down to a sad grunt. Two uniformed policemen got out of their car, and both of them drew guns.

"Freeze, hippie!"

"Hands in the air, kid."

Hoop was neither a hippie nor a kid, just a lanky thirty-year-old man with old clothes and a beard he hadn't trimmed for far too long. But he did as he was told, and just to play it safe he gave the officers a smile.

"Lean against that wall."

"Yes."

The cops holstered their guns. One officer frisked him while the other surveyed the damage in the display window with his flashlight.

"You're clean," the frisker said. "Some ID, sir?"

"Nuh,nun...ot on me."

"You're not carrying your draft card?" He shone his flashlight right into Hoop's eyes.

"Fuh,fuh,fuh,four-F," Hoop said. "Spi,pi,peach impeh,peh ...pediment."

"What are you doing here on the scene, hippie? Little looting action, that it?"

"I live here." Hoop pointed across the street. "And I work in this sssss...tore. I heard the nnnoise."

"We'll see about that," the cop answered. "And you're still required to carry your draft card at all times. It's the law."

The next to arrive was a fire truck, fully loaded and manned. Two firefighters climbed off the back of the truck, surveyed the scene, and rushed into the building carrying fire extinguishers. It took them almost no time to convert what was left of the flames into still more smoke, and what was left of the window display into a messier mess. They stomped out of the building and met with their captain, who was carrying a clipboard and taking notes.

"Cuh,cuh,cuh,call the owner," Hoop told the two police-men. "Elmer Meh,meh,meh,Maxwell. You want me to guh,go in and—"

"Stay out of the store, sir," the frisker snapped. "And you don't need to tell us how to do our job. Hey! We can do our job faster than you can say 'Jack Robinson'."

His partner laughed. Hoop did not.

Lucinda came through the front door of the store, holding a washcloth to her face and a bundled towel to her chest.

The cops were on her like doorbell missionaries. "Up against that wall, ma'am."

"Huh?"

"You heard me, ma'am. What's that you're carrying?"

"What's in the bundle, ma'am? Doing a little late-night shopping?"

"Brings you to the neighborhood? Just happened to be passing by? It's quite a hike from East Palo Alto. A little early to be doing your Christmas shopping."

"Up against the wall, ma'am," the other cop told her. "And give me that package."

Lucinda looked from one cop to the other, then back to the first. "East Palo Alto?" she said. "I don't live in *East Palo Alto*. Sir. I live in Mountain View. *Sir.*"

"And the package."

"I'll give it to him," she said, nodding at Hoop. "Sir."

The cop nodded, and Lucinda handed the bundle to Hoop. Hoop took it in his arms, but it struggled to break loose. He opened one end of the towel, and Howard Katz poked his wide-eyed head out and howled. Hoop couldn't hold on and Howard dropped to the sidewalk. Dodging the grasping hands of the two policemen, Howard dashed back into the store and disappeared in the dark.

One of the policemen said, "Aw, Christ." He rubbed a hand over his face and turned back to Lucinda. "Like I said, ma'am—"

But she held a palm up to his face and stopped him like traffic. "Here comes Elmer. You can ask him who I am. And you can ask Elmer about him, too. Save you some time."

"Did you call Mr. Maxwell?" one of the policemen asked her.

"No. I thought you called him. That's your job, right?"

"You duh,dud...on't have to tell them how to duh,do their juh,juh,dge...ob, Luce," Hoop said. "They explained that to me."

Elmer Maxwell squealed his Jaguar into the last available parking spot on the block. He got out and strode up to the unlikely gathering, a grim look on his face. When he reached them he nodded, one at a time, to each cop and then to Lucinda and Hoop. He took a deep breath and a long look at the smashed window and the smoky mess inside. He turned back and sighed. "Well, I've seen worse."

One cop said, "You're Elmer Maxwell. Am I right, sir?"

"Indeed I am."

"And this is your store?"

Elmer shook his head. "Ned Reese, you know perfectly well this is my store. You were on watch the last time my store was bombed, and the time before that. Let's dispense with the silly formalities, shall we?"

"Just doing our job, sir," the other cop said.

"And I thank you for that, Tommy Barker. But now, since you gentlemen weren't able to prevent the crime, perhaps we can work on some kind of improved surveillance program for the future. I mean—"

"What brings you to the neighborhood this time of night, sir?" Ned Reese asked.

Elmer threw his arms in the air. "Officers, my store got bombed. That's not a reason?"

"But you live in the city of San Carlos, correct?"

"Yes. Your point?"

"This bombing took place half an hour ago, tops. It takes almost half an hour to drive from San Carlos to Palo Alto. So you must have been aware this event was going to happen, if you get what I'm saying."

The other one, Tommy, said, "Did you plan this eventuality, Mister Maxwell?"

Elmer stared them both down and took his time. Then said, "I appreciate your efforts, fellows. Good work. You're exploring every possibility, and I respect that. To answer your question, I heard about this fire forty-five minutes ago. A wake-up call, you might say."

"Who called, sir?"

"Hell if I know. I'll tell you this. He had a loud laugh and no manners. Not much to go on. He wasn't particularly chatty. Hung up on me after one sentence."

"And that one sentence was?"

"'Your store's on fire, faggot,' were his exact words, I believe."

"So this anonymous phone caller was implying that you are a homosexual, Mister Maxwell?"

"That's how I took it."

"And are you, sir? A homosexual?"

Elmer laughed. "I can't imagine why that would matter. To the bomber—or to you."

The two policemen looked at each other and shrugged. Officer Barker turned to Elmer and said, "You'd be surprised, sir." Then he turned to Lucinda and said, "Anybody else in there, as far as you're aware?"

"No. Just Howard Katz."

"And who's Howard Katz?"

"You juh,dge...ust meh,met him," Hoop said. "Who's that?"

A car parked across the street, and four men approached. "Greetings," said their spokesman. "We're from the *Palo Alto Times*. I'm Art Mason, this is my colleague Bill Moore. The photographers are both named Jim."

The two Jims did not wait to shake hands but got straight to their job, flashing the scene with more unsettling light, clicking their shutters, sliding film in and out of their boxy cameras. Pictures of the store, pictures of the fire truck, pictures of the men in uniform, pictures of Elmer Maxwell, the radical bookseller, and two of his staff. The reporters took statements from Officer Reese and the Fire Department captain. Art Mason interviewed Elmer, and Bill Moore asked Lucinda and Hoop a few questions, which Lucinda slid around as best she could when it came to why she and Hoop were both in the neighborhood when the shit hit the fan. Hoop kept his mouth shut until pressured to say something, made a botch of that, and was excused.

When Luce was finished answering questions, Elmer was still going strong. "And another thing," he said. "This store will not be shut down. Not for one hour will we shut our doors, and we'll never stop selling the truth. That window display made a strong statement about the United States's immoral military presence in Southeast Asia, and people need to read about that. The display will be reassembled, and the store will not shut down. Not for one hour."

"Mister Maxwell, I'm afraid I have to interrupt at this point," Officer Reese said. "Officer Barker and I are now going to seal these premises off with yellow crime scene tape. That means no admittance until further notice. Is that understood?"

"What does that mean, exactly, 'until further notice'?"

"The detective team will be here in a few hours, I imagine. They'll probably want the place untouched all day. Maybe all weekend. Till they're finished, nobody crosses the tape. Not the public, none of your employees, not even yourself."

"Then I need to call my staff," Elmer said. "May I go inside and get my Rolodex?"

"No, sir."

"My purse is inside," Lucinda said. "May I—"

"I'm sorry, ma'am."

Lucinda began to whimper. "What about Howard?"

"Ma'am—"

"Don't you call me ma'am like that. Sir. I want you to deal with the Howard Katz issue. Do you understand me? Sir?" Lucinda knew how to stand up tall. To anybody. But she was clearly shaking.

Elmer put his arm around her shoulders. "Sweetheart, I'll make sure Howard's taken care of. Lieutenant Sanderson is a friend of mine, and he's on our side. I'll come down and talk to him as soon as he gets here. I'll tell him about Howard. Get him to be sure there's food and water. Okay?"

"I still need my purse," Lucinda answered. She turned to Officer Reese and said, "Why can't I go in and get my purse? You can come with me."

Officer Reese shook his head. "We can't tamper with a crime scene," he said.

"Could I at least get my damned driver's license and keys, so I can drive home? God."

Elmer chuckled. "Ned, c'mon. That's reasonable. For God's sake, a woman needs her purse."

Officer Barker said, "Yeah, but what if the bomb was brought into your store in that purse, Mr. Maxwell? What if that's where the bomb was hidden? See what I mean?"

Elmer laughed out loud. "In that case, there wouldn't be much of a purse left to argue about," he said. "Come on boys, let Lucinda have her purse."

After shuffling and grumbling a bit, Officer Reese escorted Lucinda into the store, and they emerged less than a minute later, Luce holding her purse in both arms, as she had earlier held Howard Katz. The two Jims both took pictures.

She said, "I'm going home. Good luck, Elmer." She turned to Hoop and said, "Goodbye, sweet thing." Then, without another word to the press or the police, she walked to the corner, turned toward the parking lot, and disappeared into the dawn.

When Hoop got back to his apartment, he found Erica Jong's *Fruits and Vegetables* was still on the kitchen table.

He stripped and walked into the bathroom, where he finally got to pee, something he'd been looking forward to ever since he woke up at four o'clock. He stepped into a hot shower and washed away the smell of smoke and sex and nervous sweat. When he came back out into the room, naked and exhausted, but still glowing from the way the night began, he realized that somebody had been in his apartment while he was in the bathroom.

The book on the kitchen table was gone.

HOW HOOPERMAN
LEARNED TO READ POEMS

"The Goops they lick their fingers,
And the Goops, they lick their knives,
They spill their broth on the tablecloth,
Oh!, they lead disgusting lives!"

Frankie took a bow.

Clara Johnson clapped and whistled. "Another one!" she begged.

"James James Morrison Morrison Weatherby George DuPree..." He recited that one, then went on to perform "The King's Breakfast," "Buckingham Palace," and "Rice Pudding." All without a stammer. He knew that book by heart.

"You're an amazing kid," his mother told him. "And I have a present for you!" She handed him a slim paper bag.

Frankie grinned, with one tooth gone. "A buh,buh,book?" He slipped the volume out of its wrapper and read the front cover aloud: "A Child's Garden of Verses."

"Shall we read it together?" his mother asked.

Frankie shook his head. "All buh,by myssss...self." He opened the book in the middle and read:

"My tea is nearly ready and the sun has left the sky.
It's time to take the window to see Leerie going by;
For every night at teatime and before you take your seat,
With lantern and with ladder he comes posting up the street.

"Now Tom would be a driver and Maria go to sea,
And my papa's a banker and as rich as he can be;
But I, when I am stronger and can choose what I'm to do,
O Leerie, I'll go round at night and light the lamps with you!

"For we are very lucky, with a lamp before the door,
And Leerie stops to light it as he lights so many more;
And oh! before you hurry by with ladder and with light;
O Leerie, see a little child and nod to him to-night!"

Clara was speechless. She had learned to control her tears, but she knew if she spoke her voice would crumble.

"You know what?"

"What, darling?"

"You're the lllamplighter, Muh,muh,Mom."

"Me? The lamplighter? Why?"

He hugged his new book to his breast. "You tuh,tuh, taught me to read!"

CHAPTER FOUR

As officer Reese had promised, the entrance to Maxwell's Books was sealed off all day Saturday with yellow tape, and a Palo Alto Police Department car was parked in front of the store. Elmer's Jag remained parked there as well, so presumably he and the detectives were cooperating inside the building. A uniformed policeman stood outside the store, shooing pedestrians on their way.

Hooperman took a long nap during the afternoon, dreaming of Lucinda Baylor and fire bombs, and was awakened by the sound of hammering. He looked out the window and saw a large piece of plywood being installed over what had been the store's plate-glass display window. The uniformed officer was removing the yellow tape, and there was Elmer, smiling and shaking the hand of a lumpy man in a brown suit and fedora.

When Hoop went downstairs and across the street, the police car was gone and he found Elmer locking the front door of his store. Elmer gave him that famous gloomy smile, the one that had filled the cover of *Time*. He shook his head and said, "If if ain't one thing, it's another." He patted Hoop on the shoulder. "And it's always something. Right?"

"Right," he agreed. "I geh,geh,guess."

"You doing anything tomorrow morning, Hooperman?"

"No puu,pup...lans," Hoop answered. "Why?"

"The investigation's over, at least as far as the store's concerned. We'll be closed tomorrow, but it's not a day off. We need to clean up the mess, so if you're available, I could use a hand."

Hoop paused. Less than twenty-four hours before he had decided that Elmer Maxwell was a paranoid petty tyrant. Hoop had also decided that he would hand in his notice before he next had to show up for work. But since that time Hoop had fallen in love. And since that time Maxwell's Books, his favorite store in the universe, had been attacked.

He said, "Cuh,cuh,cuh,count me in."

"And I'm calling an emergency meeting for two in the afternoon. The whole staff. I've been making phone calls all day, and I've reached almost everyone. I want you here, too."

"Okay. Does that mi,mi,mi,mean I'm on the sss...taff?"

Elmer grinned. "Sneaky bastard. Okay, you're on the staff. See Bernice Monday morning. She'll have you fill out the W-2. But stay in disguise, okay? Don't blab this around. We still need surveillance, and I don't want the public to know who's watching them."

"You're a sti,stit...hitch, Elmer," Hoop said.

"*Mañana*, kiddo. Wear grubbies."

"That's all I guh,got."

The first thing to notice on Sunday morning, and Hoop could notice it loud and clear from his window across the street, was that somebody had come in the night with a spray can of black paint and scrawled on the plywood façade, "COMMIE FAG."

The rest of the clean-up crew had already arrived when Hoop walked through the front door. They were in a furious boil, not so much about the bombing as about the graffiti. The only smile in the store was on Elmer's face.

"Come on, Elmer, man," Charley David pleaded. "I say let me do a full mural. I'll pay for the paint, man. Something really relevant. Gandhi, Martin Luther King, Timothy Leary type thing, you know?"

Elmer chuckled. "I appreciate the thought, pal. But the epithet stays. Believe me, it's a good thing. A reminder to the community that there's hate in the world."

"It's an insult!" Millie Larkin raged. Millie considered herself the staff lesbian—not the only lesbian, but the outest.

Elmer shrugged. "It's not aimed at you, darling. I'm the target, and I don't happen to feel insulted. Now let's get to work."

The clean-up went smoothly. The staff set up a fan and blew most of the odor of burning books and chemicals out the door. Tom Cervantes and Hoop rolled wheelbarrow loads of broken glass and burned paper through the store and out the back door, then shoveled the sad, angry rubbish into the Dumpster. Charley used a shop vac to pick up shards of litter, then took an electric sander to the surface of the display space, then vacuumed up the sawdust. Hoop laid down brick-patterned shelf paper, while Millie gathered a new crop of books to show off. She spent an hour arranging and rearranging hot fiction—writers like Kurt Vonnegut, Tom Robbins, Richard Brautigan, and Carlos Castaneda—while Elmer, Tom, Bill, and Hoop swept all the aisles and straightened the shelves. Then Elmer took the clean-up crew across the street to 'At's Amore, where he bought them a pitcher of beer and a family-size Dino Martini—Italian sausage and olives.

The meeting began promptly at two. The entire staff showed up, except for Howard Katz, who was still sulking in his counter-level cubby in the staff kitchen. They gathered in the reading area of the back room, an open space furnished with folding chairs. They arranged sixteen chairs in a circle and sat down in an atmosphere charged with angry mumbles. Hoop wanted Lucinda to sit next to him, but she didn't. She walked into the room, gave Hoop only the barest nod, and sat beside Charley David; they sat arm to arm, whispering like kids in class.

One stranger sat among the group, next to Elmer. He still wore the wrinkled brown suit Hoop had seen him in the day before. The fedora rested on his lap. He looked like a cross between Buddy Hackett and an unmade bed.

Elmer spoke. "Okay, people, let's settle down and get started, shall we? We have a lot to cover today, so I propose we dispense with the usual routines, the Check-Ins, Resentments, and Appreciations, and get right to it. Any objections?"

Mumbles. Jack Davis, the venerable anarchist, said, "Yeah. I object. For Christ's sake—"

"Overruled," said the socialist, Pete Blanchard. "I want to get home to my garden, and I don't want to spend a lot of time with encounter group games."

Elmer said, "Business first, people. Then we'll have time for checking in, if anybody wants to stay around for that."

"You're making a big mistake, Elmer," Jack said.

"Won't be my first, Jack." Elmer raised his hand for silence and the mumbling stopped. "I want to introduce a friend of mine, and a friend of the store." He nodded to the man on his left. "Some of you already know this gentleman, who's a long-time pacifist, dating back to World War Two. This is Police Lieutenant Mort Sanderson, who's in charge of investigating this crime, this bombing. I've asked him to come speak to us briefly about what's being done and what we can do to help."

Mumbles.

Tomás Cervantes said, "Wait a minute. You were a pacifist during the war?"

Lieutenant Sanderson nodded. "I'm still a pacifist."

"How can you be a pacifist and a cop?" Peggy Chao asked.

Mumbles.

Elmer held up his hand, and when he got silence, he said, "Peggy, all of you, I happen to know that Mort Sanderson is very much a peace officer."

The lieutenant spoke. "Thank you, Elmer. And thanks to all of you for showing up for this meeting. The first thing I want to tell you is that the police are on your side here. I know there's sometimes friction between, well, the counter-culture, if I can use that term, and the men and women who are paid to keep the peace. But believe me, we're on the same side. Let's work together on this, because violent crime is something we're both against." He paused for that point to sink in. He rubbed his face and went on. "The second thing I want to assure you of is that this crime originated outside the building."

Bill Harper, who took care of the Humor section, said, "Duh."

Lieutenant Sanderson nodded. "A simple conclusion, yes. But it's my job as a detective to rule things out as a first step. It appears the window was broken from the street side of the glass, probably with an axe, and then the bomb was dropped through the hole. Who did it? We don't know, but it had to be done by somebody pretty big and strong, and they had to use an axe, a maul, something like that. It's not all that easy to break a plate glass window. Baseball bat would have cracked the glass all right, but this person—or these people—had to be in a hurry. So he busted a hole, then lit the fuse, a rag sticking out of a Listerine bottle. The contents were gasoline. What we're dealing with here is your standard home-made fire bomb. Nasty."

"You keep saying 'he,'" Peggy Chao pointed out. "Could've been a woman. Ever think of that?"

"A very strong woman," the inspector conceded. "Okay. Could have been."

Jeanne McBurney raised her hand. "I have a question."

Elmer said, "Yes, Jeanne?"

"What the hell does this have to do with us?" Jeanne asked. "Is this why we had to come in here on a Sunday afternoon? I mean, I'm sad for you, Elmer, but shit. Nobody in this room bombed the damn store, so all I'm saying is can we get on with it? Does this cop have anything more to say, and then we can go home?"

Mumbles.

"Sorry to inconvenience you, ma'am," the lieutenant said, his face reddening. "But we're going to need cooperation, is what I'm trying to tell you."

"Like what?" asked Charley.

"As if the Palo Alto police give a shit about what happens to this store." Lucinda muttered, barely loud enough to reach every ear in the room.

Lieutenant Sanderson rose to his feet and scratched his cheek. "Listen, Miss Baylor—"

Lucinda gasped. "You know my name? *You know my name?*"

"The responding officer took your name, Miss Baylor. Routine. Doesn't mean—"

"How did he describe me?" Lucinda asked. "The responding officer, I mean?"

Mumbles. Mumblemumblemumble...

"People, stop it!" Elmer shot his glare all over the circle. "Mort is trying to help us out here, and I'm telling you to cooperate. Do whatever he says. He's in charge."

"My ass," grumbled Jack. But then he said, "Okay, Mort. What do you want from us?"

Harry said, "For Christ's sake, Jack. Give Mort a break here."

Mort Sanderson smiled for the first time. "Keep your eyes open is all. This guy, or this woman, whatever, is going to come back, no doubt about it. That's what they do. They come back to see if they've gotten the reaction they wanted to get. So go on about your business, which, believe it or not, I support."

"Yeah, right," Tomás said. "Excuse me, but how many books have you bought in this store? I've never seen you in here before."

Sanderson's face reddened and he cleared his throat. "I mean I support your politics, and you'll just have to take my word for that. But if you see any suspicious behavior, I want you to report it. Tell Mister Maxwell right away."

"Gotcha," said Charley, and Millie giggled. "And what are the police going to do to make sure we don't get bombed again? Don't get any more insults painted on the front of the store?"

"We're heightening surveillance," the lieutenant answered. "We're doubling the number of patrol cars cruising University Avenue during the night shifts for the foreseeable future. Meanwhile, we're on the lookout for this serial bomber. This is the third time he's hit this location, as I'm sure you're all aware. All we know about him at this point is he's strong enough to swing an axe, and he seems to hate Mister Maxwell here, for some reason. Or the store. Or what they stand for. What you all stand for. What I stand for too, by the way. Now if you don't mind, I'll be on my way, so you good people can get back to your meeting. No need to let me out; I have a key."

Lieutenant Sanderson smiled sadly, shook Elmer's hand, and shuffled out of the reading area toward the front of the store. They heard him let himself out and lock the door behind him.

Pete Blanchard said, "I move we adjourn."

"Second," said Jeanne McBurney.

Jack Davis said, "Bullshit. We don't settle questions by vote. We decide by consensus. Can I assume we all want to end this meeting?"

"You most certainly may not." This from Elmer Maxwell in all his righteous fury. The genial smile was gone. "Now that our guest is gone, we're going to get down to business. And we're not going to waste any time on protocol or procedures, because—"

"Because this isn't a democracy, man. It's a dictatorship," said Tomás Cervantes. "Right, Elmer?"

Elmer shot Tomás a glare of tired annoyance. "I'm not going to mince words," he said. "I waited until it was just us, and what I'm going to say now stays in the family. Is that clear?"

Mumble.

"Okay, then. What I want to focus on here is this. It's not just who bombed the store. Yes, that's important. Not just who wrote 'COMMIE FAG' on our lovely storefront. What interests me is *why*. Do you follow?"

No response.

"Good. Because it's just possible there's more to this than a bombing. What if this attack was just a diversion?"

"What the hell are you getting at, Elmer?" Lucinda demanded. "What do you mean, 'diversion'?"

Elmer turned to her with a squint and a grin. "Good of you to chime in, right on schedule, sweetheart. What do you have to say for yourself, Lucinda?"

"Huh?"

Silence. All eyes on Lucinda.

Elmer went on, "Tell us, please, exactly what happened Friday night and early Saturday morning."

"Huh?"

"Who bombed the store, for starters? Can you help us out there, Lucinda?"

"I don't know who bombed your damn store, Elmer. No idea whatsoever."

"Did you spend the night in the store?"

"I did not."

"Why is it you just happened to be in the neighborhood when the bomb went off, then?"

"None of your damn business."

Elmer nodded slowly, then said to Charley, sitting on Lucinda's right, "Charley, you worked the evening shift. You and Millie. Did you, either of you, see Lucinda leave the store at eleven?"

Peggy Chao jumped to her feet and shouted across the circle, "Elmer, you better stop this inquisition. You know perfectly well—"

"It's okay, Peggy," Lucinda said. "Let the big man make an ass of himself."

Peggy sat back down.

Elmer shook his head fiercely. "Charley, Millie? Did either of you actually see Lucinda leave the store at eleven o'clock? That's all I'm asking."

Charley sighed. "That's not all you're asking, Elmer, and

you know it."

Millie said, "Enough. We didn't see Lucinda leave the store. Charley and I left the store at ten. Sorry, Lucinda. Shit, Elmer, this is ridiculous."

"What's ridiculous, Millie," Elmer said, "is that I pay you to stay till eleven on Friday nights, and you and Charley leave an hour early? What's that all about?"

"I asked them to do that," Lucinda explained. "I wanted to be alone with Hoop. Okay?"

Now Elmer's wide-eyed, piercing glare was on Hoop. "My God," he said, softly, sadly. "Alone with Hoop. Okay, Hoop. Exactly what were you and Lucinda Baylor up to the night my store was robbed? I'm going to get to the bottom of this."

Before Hoop could open his mouth, let alone find words, not to mention the ordeal of voicing those words, Lucinda took care of business. With tears tracking down over her round, brown cheeks, she said, "We were in Hoop's apartment, making love, Elmer. Having sex. Screwing. What else do you need to know? How many times? What positions? How much of my private life do you think you're entitled to, big man?"

Mumbles, then murmurs, then eruptions...

Elmer held up his hand and shouted, "Quiet!" He turned back to Lucinda and said, "Darling, I apologize."

She wiped the tears with the short sleeve of her tee shirt. "Thank you."

"But I still have a couple of questions. I'll try to make this brief and kind. Okay?"

Lucinda folded her hands in her lap like a good girl and waited.

"There's still the matter of why you were inside the store when the police arrived on the scene."

"I already told you. I needed to make sure Howard was

okay."

"Howard. Okay. One other question, and then maybe we can wrap this meeting up."

"Thank God," Jack Davis grumbled.

Elmer said, "Quiet, please. Lucinda, was there another reason for entering the store in the middle of the night?"

"Huh? Before the store was bombed? Or after?"

"You tell me."

"I have no idea what you're talking about."

"I'm talking about the cash from the cash drawer that was hidden in the store—"

"That's what we always do, Elmer."

"I'm aware of that. I invented the practice. What I want to know is: did you know ahead of time that the bomb was going to go off Friday night or Saturday morning? Did you enter the store and take the sack of cash, figuring the theft would be blamed on the bomber? Or did you just see that the store had been bombed, so you took advantage of the moment, entered the store, and removed the cash and stashed it in your purse, again figuring the theft would be blamed on the bomber? Which one, Lucinda?"

The silence in the room was louder than all the mumbles and murmurs had been.

Finally Lucinda took a deep breath and blew it out in fury. "None of the above, Elmer!" she shouted. "You got a paranoia problem, you know that? Did you even *look?*"

"Of course I looked," he answered. "Are you kidding? That was the first thing I checked. I went to Bernice's cubby, found your note telling where the treasure was buried, went to the shelf, and not only did I not find the cash, I didn't even find the book."

"What?"

Elmer stood up and strode across the circle. He reached

into the pocket of his blue work shirt and pulled out a sheet of paper, which he unfolded and handed to Lucinda. "Is that your handwriting?"

She studied and paper, then looked up into his bearish face and nodded.

"Read it, please."

"'Erica Jong, *Fruits and Vegetables,* poetry.' But Elmer, this isn't where I put the money!"

"Then why did you write the note? I'm terribly confused, my dear."

"I put this note in Bernice's cubby?" She looked at Bernice, who shrugged and nodded.

"I'm sorry. I put the wrong note in your cubby. That was just a note to myself. A friend of mine recommended the book to me, and..." She shook her head and laughed. "God, what a dummy. I put the money in a different place, but I must have thrown the wrong note away. Shit." She laughed.

Elmer wasn't laughing. "Where's the money, Lucinda?"

"In Women's Studies," she answered. "Behind Simone de Beauvoir."

"Are you sure?"

"Why wouldn't I be?"

"You got it wrong last time."

Lucinda shouted, "Elmer, give me a big fat break."

Elmer Maxwell sat down and crossed his arms over that barrel of a chest. "Go get the money, Lucinda. Then maybe we can adjourn."

Jack said, "At long last."

Lucinda rose from her chair and breathed a heavy sigh of either relief or anger, it was impossible for Hoop to tell which, if not both. She left the room, saying, "Don't y'all talk about me while I'm gone."

While she was out of the room, Elmer said, "If I've made a

huge mistake here, you'll hear the most sincere apology you've ever heard, not only to sweet Lucinda, but to all of you. You people need to forgive me. As you know, shoplifters are robbing me blind, and—"

The scream from the distant front room brought Hoop to his feet. He started to go to her rescue, but Elmer stopped him with a pointed finger. "Sit down," he shouted. Hoop did as he was told.

She came slowly into the room, as if she were crossing a marble floor covered with greased b-b's. She shook her head and whimpered, through a leak of tears, "It's not there! It's not where I put it!"

The staff looked at her with sorrow. They looked at Elmer with fear. Elmer said to her, "What time do you come in tomorrow afternoon?"

"Two o'clock. I work two to eleven on Mondays."

"Very good. When you come, bring that money with you. Just put it on Bernice's desk. So we're a couple of days late with our deposit, big deal. Okay, Lucinda? If I remember correctly, the tape said it should be fourteen hundred and eighty-two dollars. Is that correct, Bernice?"

Bernice nodded. "And forty-seven cents."

"I don't care about the cents."

"Big of you," Charley muttered.

Elmer ignored him. "Bring that money back, and no questions asked. We love having you in the store, believe me. I love you, your fellow staff members love you, the customers love you. But if you don't return that cash, you can turn in your key to the store and I'll have the lock changed. Clear?"

Lucinda stood in the center of the circle, the only one standing. She clenched her fists beside her hips and whimpered, "I didn't take the money, Elmer."

"And I'll press charges."

She ran from the room, her keys rattling in her hand.

Elmer smiled and said, "I believe I heard a motion to adjourn?"

Hoop stood up and said, "I'm not ready to adjuh... adjuh,dge...ourn. This is fuh,fuh,*fuff...ucked.*"

Murmurs.

Martin West stood up, his head nodding, shaking, nodding. *"Horseshit,"* he said. *"Horseshit pigshit cowshit dogshit."*

Elmer said, "Well, Martin? You have our attention. What is it?"

Nod. Shake. Nod nod. Shake. "Horseshit. I know what's going on around here. And so does somebody else in this room." He nodded his head twice, shook it once, and left the circle, striding down the center aisle of fiction from Nabokov to Steinbeck, spouting, *"Horseshit pigshit cowshit dogshit ratshit catshit batshit...."*

HOW HOOPERMAN
MET THE LOVE OF HIS LIFE

*The kids at Fernway School didn't call him Frankie or
Frank. They called him Hoop when they were kind, or Hooperman when they wanted a good laugh. Mostly they ignored
him, unless they wanted a good laugh.*

*"Call him Hooperman!" shouted Jimmy O'Brien at recess
the first day of first grade. "That's what he wants to be
called!"*

"Hooperman! Hooperman!"

All the time Hooperman.

*Second grade, Hooperman again. The new kids needed to
be taught: "Call him Hooperman!"*

*One of the new kids didn't join in. Janie Gillis, the silent
girl with scarlet hair, who hid her mouth behind her hand,
so Frankie could never know if she was smirking at him or
laughing at him. All he knew was she was the most beautiful
girl in the universe.*

He was by her side for the first time, on the asphalt pavement when Jimmy O'Brien stuck it to him again in the usual way: "Tag—not it!"

"Not it!"

"Not it!"

And so on till the only ones left were Janie, who never said anything, and Hoop, who was always the last to say "Nah,nah,nah,nnnnn..."

Always it. They did it on purpose.

"His face is red! Look, he's crying!"

"It's a bird!"

"It's a plane!"

All together: "It's Hoooooperman!"

Frankie walked slowly back to the classroom, closed the door behind him, and sat at his desk. He picked up a book but was unable to read.

The door opened and Janie walked in. She came across the room, reached out, and touched his hot cheek, then put her finger into her mouth. Then her hand went over her mouth and she hurried back across the room to her desk, where she pulled out a sheet of paper and a pencil.

Kids drifted in, the bell rang, school lasted all afternoon, and after the last bell rang, kids ran out. The teacher left, and Janie and Frankie were the only ones left in the classroom.

Janie crossed the room and handed Frankie a sheet of paper, folded and folded and folded. She bit her lower lip. She blushed, shook her head, scurried to her desk, gathered her things, and left the room, without looking again at the boy.

He unfolded the paper and read:

"You're It"

"Your eyes are the color of sky,
Your tear has a taste of the sea,
And I keep on wondering why
You make such a difference to me."

CHAPTER FIVE

Hooperman walked into the store at ten o'clock Monday morning, as soon as Pete Blanchard unlocked the front door to let in the customers. And there was a crowd of them, some of whom looked curious, some of whom looked cautious. They tiptoed in, as if to avoid land mines under the linoleum.

Lucinda was already in the store, taking the Women's Studies section apart and putting it back together. Hoop walked over to where she was squatting in front of the lower shelves and put a hand on her head.

She sprang to her feet and whirled around, with the wide eyes of a cornered cat. "Oh. You."

"Guh,glad to see me?" he asked. "I hope?"

"Don't worry, man. I'm not shoplifting."

"Luce. I'm on your suss...hide."

"Sorry, man. I'm jumpy, is all. Now get out of my face, 'cause I got to concentrate here."

"Wh—?"

"Hoop, go away!"

"Okay. Okuh,kuh,kuk...ay." Hoop turned and walked back through the history aisle and ended up at the office door. Knocked, then pushed the door and walked in.

Bernice Rostov looked up from her desk and smiled, reminding Hoop of his Aunt Polly. Bernice had apple cheeks and she wore her gray hair in a bun that always threatened to break loose. Hoop had watched her fingers dance over the keypad of her adding machine, heard her humming while she worked.

Harry Thornton looked up from his desk, didn't smile, did the opposite in fact, and then went back to his typewriter, an ancient Underwood that supposedly had once belonged to Sinclair Lewis. He tattooed it with a couple of fingers on each hand. *Peck peck peck peck, ding swish, peck peck...*

"Welcome aboard, honey," Bernice said. "Elmer tells me you're joining our happy family. That's so nice."

Hoop grinned. "Well, it will be guh,guh,good gug...etting a puh,paycheck."

"Such as it is," Harry mumbled.

Bernice clucked her tongue. "Oh, Harry."

Harry said, "Shut up, you two. I got to get this letter off to Jack O'Leary." *Peck peck...* "Shit, Simon and Schuster didn't give us credit for the last two returns, said they were damaged, my ass, those sunzabitches are tighter than a polar bear's pucker, Christ you got to polish their knobs to get to even—"

"Oh hush," Bernice told him. She smiled at Hoop again and handed him a W-2 to fill out. He sat down on the other side of her desk and checked the right boxes, signed his name, dated the form, and handed it back to her.

"Mighty fine," she said. "It's official. You're now on the payroll. Keep track of your hours and turn them in to me every Friday. You'll be paid second and fourth Mondays of each month, and you'll be getting a dollar sixty per hour—"

"Minus withholding and all that crap," Harry added, without looking up from his typewriter. *Ding. Swish. Whir.* He yanked the paper out of the roller and separated the original from the carbon. "Damn cretins in New York. New Jersey, actually, that's where all the publishers have their returns departments, wouldn't you know. Jesus."

"Harry, wash out your mouth," Bernice scolded. "You're beginning to sound like Martin."

Harry grinned. It was the first time Hoop had ever seen the man smile. "Horseshit," he said.

Bernice faked a shudder.

"Did somebody call me?" Elmer asked, popping his head out of the Inner Sanctum. "Oh, hello, Hoop. You all signed up?" He offered his hand, which Hoop rose to shake. "Come on in my office. I need to talk with you."

Hoop followed Elmer into his office and took a chair facing the boss's desk. Elmer shut the door and sat down behind the desk. He put his fingertips together and said, "I'm giving you the night shift. You okay with that?"

Working alongside Lucinda Baylor? You kidding? "Shuh, shuh,sure. You buh,bet."

Speaking of whom, in she strutted, unannounced. She walked around the desk and slapped a cash bag down in front of Elmer. "Count it," she said.

"Where was it?" Elmer asked her.

"Count it."

"I don't need to count it. I need to know where you found it."

"In Women's Studies, like I told you yesterday. Just not behind Simone de Beauvoir. Behind Germaine Greer. I always get those two mixed up. White women all look alike.

Shit."

Elmer sighed. "Okay, darling. You can stay. But—"

"Save the but, Elmer," Lucinda snapped. "My butt's out of here. I quit." She dropped her store key on his desk, then turned, tears in her eyes, and walked out of the office without another word, never once looking Hoop in the eye.

Elmer sighed deeply and rubbed a hand over his brow, his eyes, his nose and chin. "Well, pal," he said, "looks like I need you more than ever on the night shift. I just wanted you to keep an eye on Lucinda, but now you may have to learn to run the register." He handed the key to Hoop.

Hoop pocketed the key with his mouth shut in a scowl.

Elmer said, "What? What's the matter?"

"Lucinda guhgave buh,buh,bub...fuff...ound the muh, money. She puh,puh,pup...there it *is*."

"I think she may have been letting shoplifters out without paying. That's one of their rackets, you know. So, I still want you to keep an eye on that girl."

Hoop shook his head. "She qu..." He ran out of gas, shut his mouth, and shook his head again.

"I know she quit, " Elmer said. "But you're dicking her, right? That's what she said, in front of everyone on the staff. You're dicking her."

Hoop kept his mouth shut.

"I want you to check out her apartment," Elmer said. "See what books she has on her shelf. You know what our stock is like. See if you recognize any titles. I know one thing. She hasn't bought any books from me, that's for sure. Any of my books in her apartment are stolen goods."

Hoop stood up. He fished the store key out of his pocket, dropped it on Elmer's desk, and turned to the door.

"Hoop, Hoop," Elmer said. "Be reasonable. I know this is difficult for you, but how else will we know? Believe me, I'd love to trust Lucinda, you know that. I want you to give me a reason to trust her."

Hoop spun back and fired the question. "What were you duh,duh,doing in the neighborhood Fuh,fuh,Friday nnight? Huh? And weren't you in the sss...tore all day Sss...haturday? Hmm? Isn't that tuh,tuh,true?"

Elmer's jaw dropped slowly. "Are you suggesting *I* stole the money?"

Hooperman shrugged.

"But that's preposterous."

Hooperman shrugged again. He let Elmer do the talking. Easier.

"Hoop, it's my money to begin with! Besides, how would I know where to look? And if I stole it, why would I put it back?"

Hoop was out of words.

"I hope you're not quitting, too." He held the key out.

Hoop took the key and shook his head. What else would he do? He had to earn some money. He didn't want to go back to cooking pizza.

"Good," Elmer said. "That's a relief. Have Millie train you on the register. Glad to have you on the staff, pal."

"I'm not sssspup...eyeing on Luce. Or anybody. Anymore."

Elmer laughed. "Okay. You win. I hope that includes me."

On his way to the front of the store, Hoop walked slowly through the poetry section, straightening the shelves, caressing spines, re-alphabetizing titles that had moved in his absence—a good sign, visitors were here. That's when he discovered that the copy of Charles Gullans's *Arrivals and Departures* was missing. Bummer, he thought. Somebody must have bought it. Hoop had meant to buy it himself. First edition.

* * *

Hoop spent that afternoon in the bull pen, standing behind Millie Larkin and watching her punch the register. She was efficient. She piled the purchases on the counter, one by one, with her left hand while she punched the number buttons on the register with her right. When the total showed on the register, visible to both sides, she stared at the customer with her hand out, took the cash, check, or charge card, processed the transaction and made change without saying a word or giving away a smile.

Hoop asked her during a lull, "You duh,don't tuh,tuh,talk to the cuck...ustomers?"

"I hate customers, man," Millie told him. "I consider them an interruption. Get them started and they'll talk your fucking ear off. Not my cup of oolong. If you want to talk to the customers, be my guest."

"Buh,bub—"

"Hoop, there's no rule says you *have* to have a conversation with the customers. I'm sorry if that disappoints you."

Hoop grinned. "I'm not di,di,disss...I'm relieved!"

Didn't have to talk. He would smile, because unlike Millie he pretty much liked strangers, but he didn't have to talk. That took care of worry number one.

The phone rang.

Worry number two. Hoop pulled on his beard and gazed beseechingly at Millie. She clucked her tongue, rolled her eyes heavenward, picked up the phone on the fifth ring, and said, "Bookstore."

Then she said, "Hold on." She put the receiver on top of the register and said to Hoop, "Go get a copy of *Future Shock*."

Hoop scurried to The Times They Are A-Changin' and

came back with the book and handed it to Millie. She picked up the receiver and said, "One-twenty-five." She listened to the phone a moment, then hung up.

"I'll handle the phones," she told Hoop, "if you run and fetch. Deal?"

Hoop nodded and smiled.

"Go fetch me a Coke," she said.

He saluted and left the bull pen.

In the staff kitchen, Charley David said, "Hey, Hoop, how's it going? Understand you're learning the register."

Hoop nodded.

"Millie treating you okay up there?"

"I guh,guess."

Charley laughed. "Old Millie's basically a good old girl," he said. "You just got to not let her bust your balls. She doesn't like people, is the main thing, probably because half of them are male. She hates the register. She'd rather be in the back room, fiction. Busiest area of the store, which is fine by her, because that way she can ignore dozens of customers all at the same time."

Hoop laughed. He opened the fridge and got a Coke for the basically good old girl.

Charley said, "So I guess for the evening shift it'll be you and me up front, with Millie weeding the fiction section in the back. That's the way Lucinda and I always worked. Okay with you?"

"Sure," Hoop said. "Um..."

"Yes?"

"You do phuh,phu,phufff—"

"Phones?" Charley David smiled. "I got you covered."

That afternoon Hoop walked back through the fiction aisles of the back room and knocked at the shipping room door.

No answer.

He knocked again, waited ten seconds, and tried the knob. It turned and the door opened easily. He walked into Martin West's lair.

The big Shipping and Receiving clerk regarded him with a snarl that gradually softened into a scowl and then mellowed to a look of nonchalant and nonspecific disgust. Martin nodded his bald and bearded head, cleared his throat violently, and said, "Horseshit. What?"

"Hello, Mah,Martin."

"Horseshit pigshit." Nod, shake, nod. "Hello. Horseshit. Hoop, right?"

Hoop nodded. "Martin, I wanna ask you a quh,question."

Nod. shake. Nod. "Horseshit." The big man nodded again, slower. "Yes?"

"Yesterday's mi,mi,meeting? You said you knew ss... homething? Guh,going on around here?"

Martin scowled. "Horseshit."

"I know," Hoop agreed. "What did you mi,mean, though?"

Martin squinted and shook his head. Definite No way, Go away.

"Okay."

"Horseshit, pigshit, cowshit, dogshit."

"Right. Okay." Hoop took a look around the shipping room. "You ki,ki,keep a tuh,tidy shhop, Muh,Martin."

Nod, shake. "Yah."

"Whaddya duh,do in here, anyway?"

Martin looked surprised, as if nobody had ever asked him such a personal question before. "Horseshit," he answered. "Receive shipments, get the purchase orders out, check them against the invoices, horseshit, shelve the books on the rolling bookcase. Process returns. Wrap books. Run the postage meter. Fill out the horseshit pigshit cowshit UPS book. Enter the shipments in the horseshit. In the horseshit. In the shipping log. Piles by the back door, one for the P.O., one for U.P.S. Sweep up. Shit like that." He slumped against the shipping counter, nodded his head, and sighed.

"I ask you one muh,more?"

Martin shook his head, then nodded his head, which looked the same, but Hoop could tell the difference.

"You heard about Llluci,ci,cinda?"

Nod. Shake. The snarl was back. The twitch. "*Horseshit.* Fired. Or quit. No, fired. Horseshit pigshit. Shit."

"Martin, was Lucinda stit...ealing from the sss...tore? Buh,books? Or muh,muh,money?"

Martin's face turned furious. "Horseshit!"

"Meaning?"

"Jesus! Lucinda Baylor would never steal from this store!" Martin said. "Or from any store or any person. Jesus. Shit. Horseshit, horseshit, horseshit pigshit cowshit dogshit, cat-shit, ratshit, batshit...*shit.* Get out of my office! Shit."

That evening, while Hoop was rolling Martin's trolley through the history aisles, straightening shelves and putting books away, Charley called to him from the bull pen. "Hooperman! You got a phone call!"

Panic seized Hoop by the throat. He knew for certain that he would be terrified of telephones even if he didn't have a speech impediment. He didn't have a phone in his apartment, and had avoided talking on phones since he and his wife split up. His wife had been terrified of telephones also, until she got accustomed to them, about six months before they split up. In fact, that was probably one of the reasons they...

"Hoop!"

Hoop sighed, gritted his teeth, and shuffled to the register.

He took the receiver from Charley's hand and put it to his ear. "Hoop," he said.

"Hello, dollbaby."

Oh jesus. "Um..."

"It's me, darlin. Lucinda."

"Yes, I um...I know. Um..."

"I miss you, Hoop."

"Me tuh,tut...I..." Hoop glanced at Charley, who smiled and backed away from the bull pen to give Hoop all the privacy he needed.

"Hoop, you still there?"

"I mi,mi,mmiss you tuh,tuh,tut...also, Lucinda."

She chuckled through the phone. "Hoop, baby, can you say 'yes,'?"

Hoop nodded.

"Hoop?"

"Yes. Yes, I can say 'yes'."

"Do you eat meat?"

"Yes."

"Like red wine?"

"Yes."

"You took over my shift, right? That's what Charley told me. Yes?"

"Yes."

"So you have Saturday evening off? Saturday and Sunday?"

"Yes."

"Will you have dinner with me Saturday night? My place? Huh? How about it?"

"Luce. I. You. We. I—"

"Just say 'Yes.'"

"Yes!"

"I don't want you to freak out or anything, okay? Just don't freak. But Hoop? I got a case on you, boy."

The Niagara of blood in Hoop's ears was louder than he could talk over. But he tried, oh lord did he try: "I... Luce! I mean, Guh,guh,gug...aw—I duh,dud—"

"Don't tell me, honeybun," Lucinda said softly. "*Show* me. Saturday night. Eight o'clock. Get a pencil, I'm going to give you my address."

HOW HOOPERMAN
READ FOR THE QUIET POET

They became best friends, and throughout grade school and high school they appreciated the value of best-friendship. They had their shared jokes and explosive laughs, their fierce loyalty, their painful spats, their sweet mendings. Their friendship was their strength against the fast-talking, loud-talking, teasing, inarticulate world.

It even helped them both endure the taunt: "Hooperman's got a girrrrl friend!"

When that happened, Hoop wanted to turn and shuffle away, but Janie grasped his hand, turned to Jimmy O'Brien, nodded her lovely redhaired head, and silently told the bully to fuck off and mind his own business.

Janie wrote poems every day. She practiced the art of iambs and trochees, dactyls and anapests, assonance and dissonance, rhymes masculine and feminine, and even, when she could find the discipline and patience, free verse. She wrote about nature, and about God, and about school and parents and pencils and raspberries, angels, djinns, and dragons. Bears who ate people, people who ate people, people who loved people, people who loved bears, and about a body and a mind growing up together, the joys and troubles. Poems.

She wrote them down and handed them to Hoop. To Frank. The voice.

He read them out loud.

First to her, and she wept.

Then he read them in class, and their classmates listened in stunned silence. He read them at assemblies in the school auditorium. They performed for the PTA, and for the civic clubs of Shaker Heights, Ohio.

Audiences cheered.

For Hoop Johnson, who read so well.

They all clapped for Janie Gillis, the poet!

CHAPTER SIX

Hooperman expected the week to crawl like a bug in the mud toward Saturday night, far off in the dim distance. But time did not crawl in Maxwell's Books, because the place specialized in crisis. Up and down the crowded aisles, Jack the anarchist and Pete the socialist railed all day Monday against young people, America, Nixon, and each other. Peggy Chao and Jeanne McBurney had broken up that morning, but when Hoop came on duty at three that afternoon the word was all over the store that they had disappeared together into the women's bathroom and had been closeted together for twenty minutes. Jerry Garcia was seen strolling through the aisles, playing air guitar; but since this sighting was reported by Abe Roth, it might have been a hallucination or a case of wishful thinking. A nonstop controversy filled the air for most of the afternoon about what kind of music should be piped out for the browsers: Elmer wanted classical, Abe and Tomás wanted rock, Bill and Peggy wanted oldies, and Harry insisted on *old* oldies. Bernice, in charge of the dial, went with Harry. They were of an age.

"Sorry about the music, man," Abe told Hoop, as the Andrews Sisters pleaded, "Don't Sit Under the Apple Tree" all over the store. "The Old Guard's in charge till five o'clock."

"Old Guh,guh,gug—"

"Conscientious objectors from World War II. Elmer, Harry, Jack, and Pete. Martin, too. They've known each other since they were in Civilian Public Service together, and they've all worked for the store since the beginning. They figure they've earned the right to choose the music. So, well, I'm okay with that, but come five o'clock, I promise you. Stones. The Dead. You hear what I'm saying?"

Meanwhile, Hoop became more and more a hunter. Tuesday afternoon he saw a tall, attractive middle-aged woman in the Human Sexuality section slip a copy of *Open Marriage* into her large straw purse and head toward the front of the store. Hoop took another copy of the same book from the shelf and followed her to the front, past the cash register, and out the door. Before she reached the corner, he caught up with her and said, "Meh,meh,mem...am?"

She whirled around. "Yes? What do you want?"

"I think you fuh,fuh,forgot something." He showed her his copy of *Open Marriage*.

The woman shook her head. "I didn't forget it," she said. She reached in her bag and produced the copy she had swiped. "See?"

"You fuh,forgot to peh,peh,pep—"

The woman's hand flew to her flushed face. "Oh, fuck! You're right. I *did* forget! No, that's a lie. I was embarrassed. But you're right. I'll go back in and pay for my book. Thank you, sir."

They walked side-by-side back to the store. After paying

Bill Harper at the register for her purchase, she approached Hoop with a nervous smile. She gave him a hug, breathed deeply into his bearded cheek, and whispered, "I'm so sorry. I'm so embarrassed. You're a sweetheart. Are you... available?"

At a loss for words, Hoop stepped backwards, bumping the shelving trolley against a cardboard dump of *Jonathan Livingston Seagull,* which tipped over and landed in a heap on the store floor. He stooped to pick up a handful of books, and when he turned back, the woman, her book, her handbag, and her wedding band had left the store.

Working the evening-shift register with Charley was a pleasure. Charley spoke easily, laughed gently, and listened patiently, and Hoop found that in his company he himself could speak more easily.

"Ss...ho this guh,guy guh,guh...walks into this buh,bar, and the buh,bartender says, 'What'll you have?,' and the guh,guh,guy guh,goes, 'Gi,gimme a sss...cotch and sussss... hoda, please.' And the buh,bartender guh,goes, 'That's easy for you to say!'"

After he got done laughing, Charley said, "Hoop, you did-n't stutter on that last part. The punch line. You didn't stut-ter."

"Well, see, the buh,buh,bartener doesn't ssss...tuh,tutter"

Charley shook his head. "What's the deal? You don't really stutter either? Is that it? Is this all a game?"

Hoop took a deep breath and crooned, "Many a tear has to fall, but it's all—"

"So it is an act."

"Duh,dud...on't teh,tet...ell anybuh,anybuh...anyone."

This was getting embarrassing, and Hoop was happy to see a customer, male, forties, tweedy, probably a Stanford professor, approach the register to pay for a copy of *The Berkeley Barb*.

As the customer left the store with his purchase, Millie Larkin stormed up the political science aisle, shouting out, "That asshole!"

"Who?" said Charley.

Hoop said, "Who,who,what asshole? That cuh,cuh, cuh,cust—"

"Not the customer, dipshit," Millie fumed. "That freak. In the back. That fucking *Martin!*"

"What happened, babe?" Charley asked.

"Don't call me babe," Millie said. "Martin. He tried to grope me. *Creep.*"

Charley said, "Shit. God *damn* it! I'm going to go talk to him."

"Don't bother," Millie said. She began to whimper, then shook her head, stood up straight, and said, "I'll talk to Elmer tomorrow morning. First thing. Either he fires Martin West, or I quit."

"You'd better stay up here in the front of the store," Charley said. "For the rest of the evening."

"Fuck it," Millie said, wiping her eyes with the back of her hand. "I'm going home. I don't have to put up with this shit." She came into the bullpen and found her backpack in the cavern under the register. "You guys are okay on your own." It wasn't a question. She worked her arms into the straps of the backpack and hiked it up with her shoulders.

"You want me to walk you to your car?" Charley offered.

"Forget it." With that she shuffled out of the store.

"Juh,dje...esus."

"I'm going to go have a talk with Martin," Charley said. "You okay on your own up here for a few minutes?"

"Let mi,mi,me go tuh,tuh,talk to him."

"You?"

Hoop nodded. Reaching through his thicket of beard to scratch his chin, he said, "We speak the same llanguage, Muh,Martin and I."

If Charley wanted to protest, he was interrupted by a phone call. As he lifted the receiver, Hooperman waved and walked off to the back of the store. As usual on a Tuesday night, customers were sparse, and Charley had the radio set to KABL, soporific easy listening. Perry Como singing "Hot Diggety." Hoop strolled back through Biography, past the Cliff's Notes, past the locked office door, through the open room, and on through a long aisle of fiction to the back of the store. He looked into the staff kitchen, flipped on the light, and checked out the room, which he found empty, except for Howard Katz, who was stretched out on the kitchen table. Howard opened his eyes, switched the end of his tail, and rolled over to face the other way. Hoop flipped the light off again. Then he knocked on Shipping and Receiving.

No answer. Knocked again. No answer.

He tried the door. To his surprise, the door opened easily. The light in Martin's office was on. The office was tidy. Martin was gone. For that matter, what was Martin doing in the store during the evening shift, anyway?

But the light was on. Martin must have been there.

Hoop turned off the light in Shipping and Receiving, then tried the back door of the store, EMERGENCY EXIT ONLY. It opened right up. He went out into the warm parking lot, which was empty except for Charley's weathered blue VW Bug. He looked behind the dumpsters and then up and down the alley. No Martin. No nobody. He turned back to the back door, which had closed behind him, and found it locked. At least the back door kept thieves out, even if it did let shoplifters out with their loot because the alarm was broken. Martin had broken that alarm. Proud of it.

If Martin had left the store after assaulting Millie, he was long gone now.

Hoop had a lot to ponder as he walked out to the street, turned the corner, turned again at University Avenue, and walked into Maxwell's Books through the front door.

Charley greeted him with a smile. "Can I help you with something, sir?"

"Chuh,Charley. Listen."

"So what did Martin say?"

"Listen."

"I bet he denied it."

"List—"

"Bet he said 'horseshit,' right?"

"Guh,Godduh,duh,dammit, llemme tuh,tuh,tut...alk!"

Charley clammed up and nodded. Waited.

Hoop took a deep breath. "Okay. Okay. Sss...hee, it, ss...I muh,mean shit, it's all...Muh,muh,Martin duh,duh,dud—ffuh,fuck—Mar...Mmmar...*fuck!*"

Charley put his hands on Hoop's shoulders and said, "Breathe."

Hoop took a deep breath, then blew it out and started over. "I, I, I..."

"Hoop, take your time. There's nobody around but me."

Hoop took another breath and squeezed out his thoughts. That there was no sign of a struggle in either the shipping room or the kitchen. That Martin was nowhere in the store. Left through the back, maybe. Or hadn't been in the store all evening. See, Martin didn't work evenings anyway. He left every day at quarter to five, in time to catch the bus to San Jose, where he lived. Maybe Millie Larkin was full of shit.

"You're saying Millie was lying to us?"

Hoop let the air out of his lungs, nodded, and said,

"Buh,buh,basically."

By the time Hooperman showed up on Wednesday afternoon, the word was all over the store that Martin had quit.
Bill Harper, who was cleaning up the Children's Books section, gave him the news. "You heard about Martin, right?"

"You mi,mean him and Mi,mi,Millie?"

"Millie?" Bill said. "What about Millie? Did she quit too?"

Hoop shook his head. "Sss...horry. Guh,go ahead. You
were saying?"

"Martin called in early this morning, talked to Bernice in
the office."

"Beh,bet that was some cah,cah,conversation."

Bill chuckled. "Well, Abe and I tried to get her to repeat
what Martin said. I mean in his own words. She turned beet
red and refused. But she did say Martin quit. Gave no reason,
just quit. Elmer's pissed. Martin was one of the Old Guard,
you know. Elmer wants to see you, by the way."

"Elmer wants to see mi,mi,me?"

Bill nodded.

Hoop walked back to the office. Harry Thornton looked up
from his desk and nodded, then went back to the catalog he
was scowling through. Bernice smiled. "In the back, dear,"
she said. "Elmer's waiting for you."

"What's this abuh,bout?" Hoop asked.

"Search me. Ask Elmer."

Elmer looked up and sighed as Hoop sauntered into the
inner sanctum. "Siddown," he said. "Jesus."

"What's up?"

"Hoop, I want you to take over Shipping and Receiving.
Starting Monday."

"What about Muh,Martin?"

"What *about* Martin? Except to say that he called in at

nine o'clock this morning and told me he quit. Christ al-
mighty. Try and do something for some poor schnook, and
what do they do? I rescued that guy from the Agnews loony
bin, for Christ's sake. Poor bastard, he was a human tester
during the war."

"Human teh,tester?"

"One of the options they gave conscientious objectors. Part
of the Civilian Public Service program. Pete and Jack were
smoke-jumpers in Montana, and Harry and I worked on a
farm in North Dakota. But Martin signed up to be a guinea
pig for scientific and medical research. It screwed him up
completely. And now look what he's done. He'll be back in
Agnews within a week, mark my words. He'll never make it in
the real world."

"What has he duh,duh,done?"

"He quit!" Elmer said. "I just told you that. He fucking quit
on me."

"Di,did he sss...hay why?"

Elmer threw up his hands. "Something to do with shit.
Various kinds. He majors in scatology. You know Martin. "

"Did Mi,Millie call?"

"Millie? Why? Something wrong with Millie, something
more than business as usual, I mean?"

"I guh,guess not."

"So. What about it? I want you to take over Shipping and
Receiving. Will you do that? You won't have to answer phones
back there, or deal with customers. I realize dealing with customers is hard for you."

"I want to bi,be with the bub...ooks."

"You could come in evenings, too. Be a professional
browser again, spying on shoplifters. I'd pay you for that, too.
You'd be making good money. Main thing is, we need a receiving clerk right away. Besides, you'll be greeting the books

as they come into the store. Hello, Books, Welcome aboard! We get shipments every week from Penco-Pacific, Milligan News, Book People, L-S Distributors, and Raymar, plus the publishers. I want somebody with a sense of order. Its a matter of matching invoices to purchase orders, making sure nobody's ripping us off. Can you handle that?"

"Well..."

"Hoop, one thing I forgot to say. Forgive me."

"What?"

"Please?"

"Oh. Okuh,kuh,kay."

"Thanks a million, pal," Elmer said, the peace-making grin back on his face. "I wish I had more like you on my staff, you know? Guys I can trust. Shit. Two people quitting on me in one week."

"What about the evening shift? Needs three pi,pi,people."

"I'll hire somebody. You keep the evening shift for the rest of this week. I expect we'll get a new person to start on Monday."

"Guh,gotta tuh,take cuh,care of Guh,gardening, Cuh,cook Books, Ki,kids Buh,books, Eastern Thought, Llluce's sss... hections."

Elmer chuckled. "You're a stitch, kiddo. Can't even talk straight, and you're telling me how to run my store. Well, you're right, of course. I'll get Charley to put a Help Wanted sign in the window."

Hoop nodded. "Ss...horry. Duh,didn't mi,mean to be buh,buh,bossy." He stood up.

Elmer raised his big black eyebrows, looked over the tops of his glasses, and said, "By the way."

"Yes?"

"What's happening with Lucinda?"

"Haven't ss...heen her since she qu,quit."

"I thought you two were hot and heavy. What's the deal?"

Hooperman shook his head, shrugged, turned, and left. Sometimes having a speech problem comes in handy when you don't want to answer some stupid-ass question.

UP, UP, AND AWAY!

Francis Johnson and Jane Gillis graduated together from Shaker Heights High School, on a warm June afternoon in 1960. They were the stars of their class—straight A's for four years running, both of them. They won prizes in literature, Janie for her poems, Frankie for his scholarly criticism of poetry from Homer to Frost. Both of them were published in national literary quarterlies while they were still at Shaker High.

They had been offered the titles of Salutatorian and Valedictorian, but they gladly passed the honors on to two other students who would be able to make speeches. However, they were called up to be presented with newly invented awards.

There on the stage in the center of the football field, facing the bleachers full of fans, they posed for pictures together, grinning in their green gowns and flat hats. When the pictures were snapped, they whipped off their mortar boards and sailed them over the field, turned to each other, and married their grins in a long, joyous kiss, applauded and cheered by their parents, their classmates, and their classmates' parents.

Then they looked into each other's eyes and said without words, "Without you, I'd be zero."

That evening at Guarino's Restaurant, Harold Gillis ordered champagne for them all: him and his wife, Alice; Jane and Frank; and Frank's mother, Clara. "A toast," he said, "to the greatest kids I ever met."

They grinned and sipped.

"Only one thing I don't understand," Harold went on. "I don't know why these great kids want to go all the way to California to go to college. Don't we have perfectly fine colleges here in Ohio? Just kidding, Janie, honey. You go wherever you want, but Mom and I, we're sure gonna miss our girly."

"I wonder the same thing too, Harold," Clara said. "But they have a good creative writing program out there at Stanford. It's famous, anyway."

"Well, hell's bells. Don't they have writing classes right here at Case Western Reserve? Janie?"

Janie turned to Frank and mouthed a word.

"Fullll," Hooperman told the parents. "We want to fuh,fuh,ff—"

Janie shook her head and put her hand on his before he could finish the word "fly."

"Flee," she said, in a voice as small and clear as a silver spoon on a crystal glass.

CHAPTER SEVEN

As Hooperman crossed University Avenue at three o'clock, on his way to his shift on Thursday afternoon, he could see that the plywood was gone from the store's front window and a new plate of glass had been installed. Getting closer, he could see Millie inside, busily arranging a new display of the summer's best-selling titles. When he reached the front of the store he was able to read the two signs posted in the window, next to the front door.

HELP WANTED

inquire within

Hoop stared at the second sign for a full minute, feeling the tympani in his chest, listening to the blood in his ears go over the falls.

BOOK SIGNING
Celebrate the Publication of

SOFT SHOUTS
by acclaimed poet
JANE GILLIS

Maxwell's Books
Thursday, 8 P.M., August 3

He took a deep breath, held it, and walked inside. He heard Tomás say hello to him from behind the register, but he didn't stop to nod. Instead he exhaled, gulped another deep breath, and strode down Political Science, straight through Poetry without stopping, and walked into the office.

Bernice looked up and smiled, as usual. Harry looked up and smiled, for a change. Grinned, in fact. Hoop wondered what was up with that, but didn't have time to chat and find out. He went straight to the inner sanctum door and pushed it open without knocking.

"I'm here about the ssss...hign in the window."

Elmer looked across the top of his glasses. "Hoop, if I'm not mistaken, you already have a job."

"Not that suh,sign. The other one."

"Oh, that. The poet?"

Not trusting his voice, Hoop nodded. Violently.

Elmer shrugged his face. "You'll have to talk to Harry about that. He's the one who pulled it off. He's pretty proud of himself. She's a big star, you know. Have you heard of her?"

Hoop nodded again.

"What's the matter, Hooperman? Cat got your tongue?"

"Not fuh,funny, Elmer."

"Sorry, Pal. That was a slip of the tongue," Elmer said.

"I understand," Hoop said. "That happens to mi,mi,me sssometimes."

Hoop turned his back on his boss and left the inner office. In the outer office he stopped in front of Harry Thornton's desk. Harry looked up and said, "Yes?" He was still wearing that shit-eating grin.

"Jane. Gi,gi,gig...Gillis."

The grin grew. "Isn't it great?" the buyer said. "Finally a big-name author! We'll pack the house! We'll sell a zillion copies!"

"We'd better," Bernice said. "We already owe Farrar Straus a bundle."

"Isn't it great?" Harry repeated.

Hoop nodded. "Guh,great. I guh,guess."

"Hey," Harry said. "I understand you're taking over Shipping and Receiving."

Hoop nodded.

"Elmer asked me to teach you the ropes back there. If you have time right now, we could go back to the shipping room and I'll show you the routine." Harry stood up. "Shall we?"

"Okay."

The lesson took only fifteen minutes.

Receiving: open the package and find the purchase order number on the invoice; pull the store copy of the P.O., which is kept in the wire basket in numerical order; check the books received against the invoice, and check the invoice against the P.O.; stack the books on the shelving trolley; give the paperwork to Bernice. Save the carton and the packing material if they can be reused; the rest goes in the Dumpster outside.

Shipping: find the returns packing list and label in the out basket and match them with the books on the shelves, pack the books and include the packing list; apply the label; weigh the package; run the postage meter or fill out the UPS book page. Here's how.

"That's pretty much it," Harry said. "Simple enough, right?"

"Guh,got it. What about the shh,shipping log?

"Shipping log?"

"No sh,shipping log?"

Harry shook his head. "No shipping log. I keep a copy of all the packing lists. Millie goes around during her evening shift and collects the books from stock to be shipped out the next day. She marks up both copies of the packing list—yours and mine—if we don't have the books ordered. That hardly ever happens, though. Most of the books you'll be shipping out are returns, and I've already counted the quantities on the shelves."

"Okuh,kay."

"You'll get the hang of it," Harry said.

"Qu,question."

"Hmm?"

"When is that new Gi,gi,Gillis book cuh,coming out?"

Harry beamed with pride. "Official pub date is September first, but we'll have copies by the first of August. Sooner, in fact. I ordered two hundred. She's sort of a celebrity around here, because she went to Stanford and earned a bunch of awards. Our store is the first venue on her tour! The Farrar Straus and Giroux rep, Alan Kishbaugh, promised me that."

"Guh,good for you."

"Alan had FSG send me an advance reading copy. Nice cover. Nice picture of the poet too. She's a looker, that's for sure."

"That's for sure," Hoop echoed.

"You like poetry, right, Hoop? You want to borrow the book? I took it home, but I could bring—"

"No thanks."

"Well, there will be plenty of copies come August. And you'll be the first to hold one in your hands. Think of that!"

Hoop nodded. "Think of that," he said.

And that is all Hoop thought about for the rest of the afternoon and into the evening, while he punched the keys on the register, while he fetched books from the shelves, while he apprehended four thieves in the act of ripping off books. And all night long, while he didn't sleep. And all day Friday, while he couldn't read in the morning. And back at work for the evening shift, his last, on a Friday night, always the busiest night of the week once the Varsity Theater let out after the early show. The customers were a blurred parade of nobodies while he thought. He thought, with a dreadful chill, of Janie walking back into his life, even if only for one terrifying evening.

Time to plan a vacation. Sick leave.

He'd talk to Elmer about it first thing Monday morning. Elmer would be patient while he spilled the beans, spilling broken words all over the desk.

Elmer would understand.

Saturday morning, a little after eleven o'clock, Hoop walked into Easton's Coffee Shop, up University Avenue from the bookstore. He reached into a booth and grabbed a *Palo Alto Times* that had been left behind by a customer, then took a seat at the counter. He ordered his usual Saturday morning fare, two eggs over easy, hash browns, sausage, and dry wheat toast, and wondered, as usual, why he never ordered anything fancier, or even different. He found himself wondering if Janie still ordered the same thing every time she ate breakfast in a restaurant, sunny side up with bacon and rye toast, or had she moved on and moved up to eggs Benedict, or caviar omelets, or salmon *à la ooh-la-la* for brunch at the fucking Ritz, if you please. Best seller. *Star.*

He read the *Times* while he waited. Jane Fonda was still vacationing in North Vietnam. George Carlin had been arrested the night before for saying seven dirty words in Milwaukee. The nation was split down the middle, it seemed, between uptight fascists and ill-mannered anarchists. "And I cuck ould gug ivashit," Hoop mumbled aloud, to nobody. When his breakfast was plopped before him, he folded the paper and left it for the next customer to come along. As he ate his eggs over easy, not as easy as usual this Saturday, he tried to remember the headlines on the front page of the *Times* and found that the news was gone from his mind. By the time he was done mopping up the yolk with the last of the hash browns, he was back thinking about the third of August.

Less than two weeks away.

To be here, or not to be here? Good question.

Maybe just hang out in the back. Get a load of her, all dressed up. Smiling that way. Listen to her voice. See who's touring with her, coaching her.

If it's still Robin, I won't stick around to shake his hand, Hoop thought. Shook that hand enough. Silver-tongued son of a bitch.

He got up from his stool, pulled some money out of his pocket, and left two-fifty beside his plate. As he turned toward the door he noticed, there on the same table where he'd snagged the *Palo Alto Times,* a copy of—*the* copy of, Hoop was certain of that—*Arrivals and Departures,* the Charles Gullans book that had gone missing from the Poetry section a couple of weeks earlier. He stopped at the booth and put his forefinger on the book, then looked into the face of the customer who was waiting for his breakfast.

Same guy. The man he'd caught stealing the Adrienne Rich book, his first week on the job. Same wispy beard, same soiled and wrinkled linen jacket.

"You sss...tole that buh,buh,book," he said. "Lawrence Hal-deman."

The man shook his head fiercely. "Holgerson. And I most certainly did *not*. Steal that book."

"Then why is it mi,mi,missing from the sss...store? You peh,paid for it?"

"I haven't been inside that store since you accused me of stealing that other book," the wimpy-bearded little creep said. Baldfaced liar. "I wouldn't set foot in Maxwell's Books if you paid me. Now get your greasy finger off my book. That's a first edition."

"I know." Hoop lifted his finger from the book and pointed it at the man's face. "Where did you guh,gug,get it, then?"

"I use a mail-order book scout," Holgerson said.

"Got a reci,ci,ci,ceipt?"

"As a matter of fact, I do." He pulled a half-sized sheet of yellow paper from between the pages of the book and handed it to Hoop.

It was a generic sales slip, the kind sold at stationery stores. A rubber-stamped name at the top read "R.C. Book Dealer." There was no address. The record of the sale was typed below:

1 – Gullans: Arrivals and Depart ures,
First Edit ion, mint .
$14.00
PAID, 7/7/72

Hoop handed the receipt back and asked, "Who is this R.C. Book Dealer? What's the address?"

"That's none of your damn business," Holgerson an-swered. "What's the matter with you, hippie? You having a bad hair day or something? Now leave me the fuck alone."

Hoop thought a minute.

Trouble was, Hooperman *was* having a bad day. He let out his breath in a sad sigh and said, "Sss...horry. Enjoy the buh,book. I apah,pologize."

"Fuck off."

"Have a nice duh,duh,day."

Hoop decided to take his own advice. He went back to his digs over 'Ats Amore, rolled himself a number, put it into his Sucrets box, and trotted back down the stairs. He hiked off into the streets of Palo Alto, wandering through the tree-lined streets and avenues, among the brown-shingled houses of Professorville, until he reached Rinconada Park. He found a eucalyptus tree to lean against, far enough away from people to fire one up, and he sat with his back against the bald and fragrant trunk. He lit the joint, sucked the smoke, held it in, and blew it out.

Again.

Again.

That's better. He wet his fingers and pinched the coal, then dropped the roach into the tin box and snapped it shut.

He stood, pocketed the box, and wandered around the park, listening to the *ponk, ponk* of a tennis game, the shrieks and squeals of toddlers on slides and swings, the arguments of jaybirds, *the whshhhh-tsh tsh tsh* of a sprinkler.

He set out awandering. He walked the tree-lined streets of Palo Alto, getting lost, then found, then lost again, until finally he found himself at the San Francisquito Creek, where he stood on the Pope Street Bridge, with one foot in Menlo Park.

And everywhere he went he thought to himself, She and I walked here together. She wrote a poem about this tree, this house, this bridge, this town.

What the hell am I still doing here?

But I live here. This is my home. She's the one who left, not me.

So why didn't she just stay away?

When he returned to his room, Hooperman was sweaty, tired, and hungry. He looked forward to a shower. A nap. And for dinner? Could he stand to eat pizza again? Third time this week?

As he was undressing he found the note in his jeans pocket, the one he'd been carrying around since Monday.

3129 Easy St. Mt. View. F

Oh God.

Oh God good? Or Oh God bad?

Hoop didn't know for sure. All he knew for sure was that he'd have to get back into his rust-colored VW Bug, which was parked behind the pizza parlor, and hope that the damn thing still worked. He hadn't driven for more than two weeks. And that was just to the Launder-Net.

He stepped out of his jeans and threw them onto the pile on his closet floor. Okay, he thought. Time to regroup.

If I'm going to Lucinda's for dinner....

Since I'm going to go to Lucinda's for dinner tonight, it's time to go to the Launder-Net this afternoon. He checked his wallet. Ten bucks. Enough for laundry, and while the laundry was cooking, enough left over to go to Lucky's across the street and buy a nice bottle of red wine and a bunch of flowers.

But first the shower. Then the nap.

When he lay down on his bed and shut his eyes, he thought, It'll be good to see her again. Lucinda.

But the face he saw smiling back at him was Janie's.

HOW HOOPERMAN AND JANIE WATCHED THE SETTING SUN

Hoop and Janie stood alone together on the top of the ridge, on a warm evening in May, looking west at the sun resting like a deflating red balloon on the edge of the sparkling Pacific Ocean. When they turned and looked behind them, they could see the Bay, and the cities along the Bay starting to turn on their lights for the evening. The field around them was green-turning-gold, waving in the suddenly cool breeze, and Hoop wrapped his arm around Janie's shivering shoulders.

The sun flattened out more.

He said to her, "Meh,meh,meh,married." Meaning: We're going to get married! At the end of the summer, in Shaker Heights, and our families will be there, and they'll rejoice, and we'll be married! Married! Man and wife!

She faced him. She reached up and put her hand on his

cheek. She nodded. She said, "Home." Meaning: And we'll have our own place! Our own. We'll live together in married student housing for our senior year, and we'll have our own kitchen and our own living room, and our own bedroom, and our own bed. I'll cook for you. You'll shop for me. I'll clean the house. You'll do the laundry. And together we'll make each other so, so happy!

He said, "Fuh,fuff...uck yes!" Meaning: Yes, and we'll do it, make each other happy in the mornings and at night and all night and sometimes in the afternoons when you're not too busy writing....

"Look," she whispered.

They held hands and watched the soft sinking sun as it flattened out and separated into stacked crimson disks and settled down below the bottom of the sky.

"Bink. All gone."

"Buh,bonk," Hoop agreed. "Hungry?"

"Mmm."

They got back into the red Volkswagen and drove to the Skyline Lodge, where they played the jukebox and danced, ate steak and drank wine, and promised in joyful silence to love each other for all the days of their lives.

Then they drove down the mountain to Hoop's basement apartment in East Palo Alto, where they practiced and re-practiced the way and all the other ways they would make each other happy all the nights of their lives.

"Time." Meaning: You have to take me back to the dorm now, or we'll be in deep shit.

So they left the apartment and drove to the campus, and in the parking lot he put his hand on her bosom and said, "Pillowed upon my fair love's ripening breast, to feel forever *its soft fall and swell, awake forever in a sweet unrest, still, still to hear her tender-taken breath, and so live ever, or else swoon to death."*

She whispered, "Good night, my silly."

CHAPTER EIGHT

Easy Street was easy to find. So was 3129. The apartment complexes on Easy Street all looked the same, but the number was on the front of Lucinda's building, giant iron numerals lit by a spotlight. Hooperman parked his VW on the street, got out, and walked to the passageway into the complex, carrying his wine and roses.

Apartment F. "F as in love," she had told him on the phone. He could have used logic or a directory to locate Apartment F, but, nervous as he was, he decided to just wander the walkways of the complex, looking for love. He found F on the second floor, in the back. Curtains were drawn, but the apartment glowed with soft light.

He rang the bell. Heard the footsteps. Bit his lip.

The door opened, and there she stood, wearing a warm smile. Wearing a hippie gown, some long thing with little mirrors all over it. "You came," she said softly. "I was worried."

He nodded and held his gifts out to her, over the threshold, one in each hand.

"For me? Oh, Hoop! You didn't have to do this! Wine! Roses?" She took the gifts and held them to her bosom.

Hoop grinned. "Laugh and run away," he recited, "like a child at play through a meadowland toward a closing door, a door marked 'Nevermore,' that wasn't there before."

Lucinda shook her head and said, "You're a nutcase. Get in here, you. Let me put these in the kitchen so I can give you a huge, huge hug."

Hoop followed her through the living room—thrift store furniture, Modigliani poster tacked up on one wall, the stereo playing Ella Fitzgerald, "Knock on Wood"—to the kitchen, where she set the flowers and the bottle on the counter. The garlicky, oniony, herby smell of simmering pasta sauce complemented the hefty, happy brown woman who walked into his arms.

"I've missed you, dollbaby," she murmured.

"Me tuh,tuh,too."

"Let's open that wine up." She read the label. "Petit Syrah. Cool. Here's a corkscrew. You do the honors, while I give these posies a drink." She handed him the bottle and the corkscrew and scrounged in a lower cupboard for a jar big enough for the bouquet of small roses. When the flowers and the bottle were on the kitchen table, breathing in and out, and the sauce was bubbling gently, Lucinda took Hoop's hand and led him back to the living room, where they sat down on the lumpy couch, one at each end.

"Nice puh,puh,pup...lace."

"I gotta get me a job pretty soon," Luce said. "So I can afford this place. Besides, I'm getting lonely. I been missing you, Hooperman."

"You think Elmer muh,muh,might rehire you?"

"Hell with Elmer," she said. "I'd rather wait tables. Be a

bank teller. Or go back to modeling. I'm going to get us a glass of wine." She stood up and walked to the kitchen.

When she returned, bottle in hand, she placed two wine glasses on the coffee table, on straw coasters like the ones he and Janie had bought at Cost Plus.

She filled their glasses, set the bottle on the table, and sat down, closer to him this time. They clinked and sipped. The little glass mirrors on her dress winked at him.

"Nice," she said. "You're so sweet."

"You were a muh,model? Are?"

"Not a fashion model, if that's what you're asking. I used to model for all the art departments around. Stanford, De Anza, La Cañada, Foothill, Santa Clara, and some private groups, too. Adult ed, Jewish Community Center, and stuff. They seem to like my fat black body. Who knows why. All I know is the pay's good, ten dollars an hour. Trouble is getting the gigs. I used to belong to the Palo Alto Model's Guild, but I quit when I started working for the bookstore. Shit. Maybe they'll let me back in. *Shit*. I'm doing all the talking. Am I nervous, or what? Come on, Hoop. You talk for a change."

Hoop took another sip. "That *would* be a chuh, chuh,change."

"Or we could just sit here. Hold hands? Listen to the music?"

Ella: "Yellow Man."

They tried sitting quietly, gulping through two more glasses of wine, but Hoop began to fidget, and Lucinda's peaceful smiles grew more and more forced. "So," she said, as Ella moved on to the next number, "how's things at the store? I saw that poster in the window—Jane Gillis! Coming to Palo Alto! God, Hoop, you must be stoked!"

"I geh,guess."

"She's your favorite poet, right? I mean, you know her *per-*

sonally. God."

"Used to," Hoop said. "While aguh,go. In cuh,cuh,college."

"But she signed those books to you. Hardbacks. That's heavy stuff."

"I guh,guess."

"Was she your girlfriend?"

"Muh,muh,muh,muh...more."

"How much more?"

Oh hell with it, Hoop thought. She'll find out anyway, eventually. "A doll in a teacup she were. But we lived on the square, like a true married pair, and I learned about women from her."

They sat in silence, until Lucinda took a deep breath and let it out. "Maybe we'd better change the subject," she said, fingering one of the mirrors on her chest.

Hoop gave her a tentative smile and a confident nod. Yes, please. "Ss...ho, you like Erica Juh,juh,dge...ong?" he asked.

"How did you guess?"

"You buh,borrowed that buh,book, that night. *Fruits and Vegetables*. Fuh,from the sss...tore."

She nodded, still not smiling. "Right. Yes. Yes I like Erica Jong a lot. I wish she'd write a novel. Want some more wine?"

Hoop nodded.

She refilled their glasses, finishing the bottle. "Come to think of it," she said, "I'm starting to get hungry. How about you? You want to come toss the salad while I cook the pasta? And I got garlic bread in the oven. How's that sound?" She rose to her feet.

"Wonderful!" He stood up.

"I didn't make you a dessert. I don't know how."

Hooperman took the big woman in his arms and whispered to her ear, "You'll buh,be all the dessert I want."

She squeezed back, and in a little, little voice, she said, "I love you, Hoop." She cleared her throat and quickly added, "I mean, I've *missed* you so. You know?"

Ella sang: "I'll never fall in love again...."

Dinner was delicious and nearly silent. He asked her questions like, "Oregano?"

She answered, "Mmm."

They drank the last of their Petit Syrah, and Luce got up and hauled a jug of Red Mountain out of the fridge and filled their glasses. They slurped linguini and crunched lettuce.

Hoop told her he was in charge of Shipping and Receiving now. No longer a store sleuth. Also no more telephones.

"Congratulations," she said. "You get to be Martin."

"Horseshit, pi,pi,pigshit."

She laughed and red wine sprayed from her nose.

More silence.

The music stopped. Lucinda stood up and said, "I'll put something on. What do you like? You like Aretha?"

"Guh,got anything sss...hofter?"

"Whiter, you mean?"

"No. I di,di,didn't mean that. Not at all."

"Sorry," she said. "Just kidding. Bad joke. Hoop, forgive me. I'm nervous. How about Brubeck?"

"You have Buh,Brubeck?"

"You sound surprised."

"Which album?"

"I don't know the name of it, actually. Somebody left it here. I mean—"

"It's okay, Luce. Sss...hit down. We don't nneed any music. Guh,great spagheh,ghetti!"

"Linguini."

"Right."

"Same thing, actually. Honest to God, why did I do that?

Correct you? Shit. Sorry Hoop. I'm sort of weird tonight."

Hoop put his hand on hers. "Fi,fi,finish your puh,pasta. I'll wash the di,dishes."

She brightened. "Forget the damn dishes, honeybunch. I got designs on your bod. And guess what."

He grinned: *what?*

"I got a candle in my bedroom. Wanna see it?"

"I wanna see *you*."

"Okay," she said. "So long as you don't peek."

"Preteh,teh,tend I'm an artist. Muh,model for me."

As they stood up and she took his arm, she said, "This is more like it. Huh?"

"You're all cuh,cuh,candlelight," he told her, as they lay on the low bed, still wrapped in too many clothes. "Little ss...pots of light all over you!"

She fingered two mirrors, one on each breast. "You like this dress?"

"Yes, but...."

"But?"

"Let's tuh,tuh,tuh,take it off!"

"Close your eyes, then. I'll blow out the—"

"No. Luce. Puh,please!"

She sighed. "You first."

"No puh,problem." He kicked off his sandals and let them tumble to the floor, unbuttoned his shirt and pants, peeled away his clothes, and tossed them across the room into the dark. He sat up cross-legged on the bed, turned to her, put a trembling hand low on her belly, and said, "Your turn. You want some help with that duh,duh,dress?"

"I'm nervous, Hoop."

"I'm nervous, tuh,too."

"Lucinda rose from the bed and stood looking down into

his gaze. She smiled shakily, then put a hand behind her back. Hoop heard the zipper slur, then watched her shimmy her shoulders, then her hips, as the mirrored gown slid down and fell like sparkly rain to the floor. Her body was round and brown and quivering. She flicked her black nipples with her thumbs, then rippled her fingers down over her belly to the black mat, combed her fingernails shyly through her fur, then bent her legs until her knees rested against the side of the bed.

She smelled like cinnamon.

She leaned to the side and blew out the candle. Darkness dropped on the room like a warm, starless night. *Cinnamon and honey.*

God...

"Ready or not," she called in a whisper across the distance, "here I come!"

"I'm ready."

After a long while in the still and silent dark, Hoop let out the breath he'd been holding and muttered, "I guess I'm not ready after all. Shush,hit."

"It's okay, baby," Lucinda murmured. "Let's just hold each other and relax. See what happens."

After another long, tense and unsuccessful cuddle, he began to tremble. "Sss...horry," he whimpered.

"It was the wine, maybe," she offered. "Just try to relax, okay?"

Just as he was learning to breathe again, he heard her say, "Hoop?"

"Mmm?"

"It's none of my business, but that poet? Jane Gillis?"

He gritted his teeth. "Mmm?"

"Were you lovers?"

Hoop squirmed out of her hug and sat up on the edge of the bed. "It was a long tuh,time ago, Luce."

"Were you married? You were, weren't you?"

He didn't answer.

"You still have any feelings?"

"Anger."

She paused a moment. "That's another word for love," she told him. "And now you're going to get to see her again. How will that be? Huh?"

Hoop stood up. "I'm sss...horry," he said again. "I'm afuh,fraid I'm.... I...." He ran out of things to say.

"Lay back down," she said. "Beside me. Please, Hoop. I got too personal. I'm sorry."

He took another deep breath. "It's easy to get puh,puh, personal at a tuh,time like this," he said. "I think I'd better guh,go."

"You mean that's it? *It?*"

"You mind if I tuh,turn on a light? I mean, to get duh, dressed?"

"Okay, sure. Switch by the door. Just keep your eyes on the road."

"I'm sss...horry, Luce."

"Oh, shut up and dress. We're still friends, man."

Hoop stumbled across the candlelit room, found the door and the light switch, which made the room bright, and small, and hugely unfamiliar. He glanced in her direction. She lay on her back, staring at the ceiling. She wasn't hiding a thing, but Hoop was done looking.

He picked up his shirt and slid his arms into the sleeves, then buttoned up. Then he found his undershorts. Pulled them on. He shook out his jeans, sat on the foot of the bed, and pulled them on. Stood up and slipped into the sandals.

He found he was facing a bookcase full of new books, most of them paperbacks, all of them familiar. There it was. He walked right to the center of the middle shelf and pulled it out.

"What?" she called from the bed. "What are you doing?"

"*Fruits and Vegetables,*" Hoop read. "The book you buh,buh,borrowed from Maxwell's Books. Right?"

"Are you accusing me of...what? You still a bookstore cop, man? I thought you gave that shit up."

He turned and looked at her. She was propped up on her elbows, no longer hiding her flesh from his sight, but he wasn't looking at her flesh. He looked straight at those defiant eyes and said again, "Right?"

She stood. She picked up her dress, then said, "Fuck it," and let it fall. She turned to him and said, "I was going to give it back, but then Elmer fired me, and I figured, shit, that fucker owed me at least that much. You going to bust me? Aw, shit, Hoop. Take the damn book, give it back to Elmer. It's not that big a deal. The world's ruled by assholes, and you might as well play on the winning team. Now why don't you just—"

"These other buh,buh,buh,books? You were going to return them, tuh,too?" He took a deep breath and let it out. "Luce," he asked as calmly as he knew how, "Are you running a buh,buh,bookstore here? Are you a buh,book ss...cout?"

"What the hell are you talking about? Hoop? What's going on?"

"*Arrivals and Departures,* by Charles Guh,Gullans? Did you take that one, tuh,too? Sss...ell it to Holgerson?"

"I never heard of it. Never heard of the book, never heard of Holgerson, whoever that is."

"I see."

She flared her eyes, strode by him to her closet, and

whipped a robe around her body. She stood in front of him and said, "Hoop, you innocent child, we *all* do it. All of us. Everyone who works at the store takes home books. We're careful with them, and when we're finished reading them, we bring the books back."

Hoop pointed at the bookcase. "All of these?" he asked. "You were going to retuh,tuh,turn—" He closed in on the bookcase and read the titles on one shelf: *"Another Roadside Attraction, Trout Fishing in America, Cat's Cradle, The Pentagon Papers, Journey to Ixtlan—"*

"I haven't read them yet. I'm a slow reader, okay? I didn't go to college, like you. You and your famous girlfriend. Ex-wife. Shit."

He shook his head.

"Tell you what," she went on. "Bring some boxes over here, and we'll pack up these books and you can take them back to the store, and nobody will be the wiser. I know I kept them longer than I should of. I admit that. Okay?"

"When?"

"Tomorrow?"

"They won't all fi,fit in my VDud...oubleyou."

She laughed. Out loud.

"I know. I tut...alk fuh,funny."

"You *think* funny, Hoop. How about you bring me some boxes tomorrow, and we can pack the books up and you can take some of them and then I'll bring some of them in my car, and we'll drive them to the back door of the store, and whatever?"

"Not my puh,problem," Hoop said. "I'm not the store cuh,cop anymmore."

"I was just asking for a favor, Hoop," Lucinda said. "Why are you so damned angry? Jesus."

Angry? Maybe. No, hurt. No, embarrassed. No, just God

damned eager to get out of this room with a woman he liked so much he couldn't stand being with her another minute. "I gotta run."

She nodded and put a hand on his shoulder. "Run, then, sugar," she said. Her smile had turned south. "And if you ever think of running back this way, call me first, okay? To be sure I'm not seeing somebody else by then? Somebody real famous maybe? Somebody with a little more oomph? More self-esteem?"

Jesus.

Hoop turned away. Just before he reached her front door, he heard her say, "Hoop?"

He stopped.

He heard her say: "One more thing."

He turned. She approached him until she stood a slap away. But it wasn't a slap. She walked even closer and kissed his bearded chin. "Dollbaby," she said. "Thank you for my roses."

KUK...RYPTONITE

Jane Gillis Johnson's verse play, Loud and Clear, *which she had written throughout the fall and winter quarters of her senior year, was produced at Stanford's Dinkelspiel Auditorium the evening of May 21, 1964. Frank and Janie sat in the front row of the audience, holding hands, listening breathlessly to every perfect line. The actors projected their voices, and the rhymes and rhythms of her words filled the hall, calling forth laughter, shocked silence, and in the end a tide of applause as the lights dimmed to black and then returned for the cast to take their bows.*

And their second bows. Hoop stole a glance at his wife and saw her engulfed in a glow of praise as she wiped tears of relief from her eyes with her knuckles.

Robin Clarke, the director of Loud and Clear *and the star graduate student in the Speech and Drama department, walked in front of the actors and held up his hands for silence. He said:*

"Thank you, ladies and gentlemen. Do I hear anyone call

'Author, Author!'"

The audience shouted back, on cue, "Author! Author!"

Janie squeezed Hoop's hand, smiled gently at him, and said, out loud, "Oh dear." She rose from her seat, walked to the side of the proscenium, and trotted up the steps. She crossed to center stage, where she kissed Robin Clarke on the cheek, and then stood next to him, holding his hand. They bowed together. Then a bouquet of roses appeared from nowhere, and Robin placed them in her arms.

Once again he held up his hands for silence.

When the auditorium was quiet, he said, "Jane? Do you have anything to say to your fans?"

Jane took a breath. She bit her lower lip. She buried her face in the roses for only a moment, then grinned into the spotlight. After a tense pause, she said, projecting her voice to the back of the auditorium, "Thank you! Thank you all. I thank this marvelous cast, I thank my teachers in the Writing Program, and I especially want to thank the director, Robin Clarke, my wonderful voice coach, who has worked so hard on this play, and who has worked so patiently with me and has taught me to speak out loud. Loud and clear!"

This time he was the one kissing her cheek, to the sound of more applause.

Robin said, when he had their attention again, "Please join us next door, upstairs at Tresidder Union, for a reception provided by the Writing and Drama departments. And after that, we're having a no-host Loud and Clear cast party at Ricky's Hyatt House. Jane and I will be there, and you're all invited. Right, Janie?"

"Right! Oh, and I also wanted to thank my husband, Francis Johnson, for being so patient with me during this amazing year, and...."

Those were the last words Hoop heard as he left the audi-

torium.

He had seen it coming, all year long, and now here it was. They had talked it over. For the best, she said. She and Robin had both received fellowships at the University of Michigan for the following year. They were already writing a play, together.

Jane Gillis's second book of poetry had already been published by Norton, and she had won a grant from the National Endowment for the Arts. She had not won the Guggenheim fellowship, but had been advised to try again next year.

Loud and Clear was scheduled to be produced the following year at the Ashland Shakespeare Festival and the Pasadena Playhouse.

Self-confidence had made her stunningly beautiful. More beautiful than Hoop had ever seen her be.

Hoop walked out of Dinkelspiel Auditorium, into a misty night. Scratching his six-week-old beard, he trudged back to married student housing, on the far side of the campus, and began packing his books into boxes. His books, not hers. Her books, and the books that were theirs, he left on the shelves.

He had already quit going to classes.

Why bother to graduate?

Why bother to bother?

Fuh,fuh,fuff...uckit.

CHAPTER NINE

When Hooperman walked into the Shipping and Receiving room to start his new job on Monday morning, he saw that his supply of cardboard cartons was depleted and his sealing tape dispenser was missing. He found an envelope on the counter, with his name on it. He tore it open and read:

"Hoop, I'll bring everything back Monday night. Be here at eight? Just don't tell Elmer about this, okay? I'm trusting you. I mean it. L."

Fine, Hoop thought, except for the missing tape gun. How was he supposed to wrap packages? That was his job: wrap packages. He went to the out basket and saw that it was empty. No shipping to do. *Okay, then. Okay for now,* Hoop thought.

That wasn't the real problem anyway, and Hoop knew it. The problem: he'd have to face Lucinda Baylor that evening at eight, have to let her in the back door, have to take all those stolen books off her hands and put them away on the shelves, and that was going to be a pain in the ass, and...

No. The problem: he'd have to face Lucinda Baylor that evening at eight. Knowing she'd be knowing what a sorry excuse for a lover he was.

Wanting another chance and knowing he'd never ask for it because he didn't deserve it; and besides, who's to say he wouldn't make a damn fool of himself again? Another flop in the sack.

"Be here at eight," she says. We'll see about that, Hoop thought. *We'll just see about that.* And he knew he'd be there at eight. Knew he'd be there early.

Because, and here was the worst part. The worst part. Hoop had fallen in love again, for the second time in his life.

Hoop went into the staff kitchen for a cup of coffee. Tomás Cervantes was seated at the table, flipping the pages of the new *Penthouse.* He looked up and said, "Hey, man."

"Hey."

"Just catching up on my current events," Tomás said. He closed the magazine. "So, guess who was in the store yesterday."

"Llll—"

"You got it. You two still hot and heavy, man? She's some chick, man."

Hoop shrugged. "She is," he said. "We're not." Hoop held a mug under the spout of the coffee urn and drew himself an inky, stinky brew. "Yesterday's?" he asked.

Tomás said, "Probably. Or Saturday's. Nobody makes fresh on the weekend. Peggy usually takes care of the coffee in the mornings, but she called in with cramps this morning. Guess who else was in the store."

"I gi,give up."

"David Harris. Joanie's old man?"

"How was Duh,David?"

"Stoned. Got into an argument with Pete about socialism. Pete thinks you have to be over fifty to be a socialist. David called him a dinosaur, so Jack laughs and says he's right, then David calls Jack a Tyrannosaurus rex, and Pete laughs, and David buys a copy of *Daybreak* and leaves."

Hoop unplugged the urn, poured out the sludge, and washed the insides out. He emptied the boggy, black basket, rinsed it out, and filled it with Yuban, then filled the urn with cold water. He plugged the urn back into the wall and turned on the switch.

"You're handy around the house," Tomás observed.

"Yup."

"You're a man of few words, Hoop."

"So I've been tuh,tuh,told." Hoop headed toward the door.

"No offense. I just meant, you know, like, well, you know." Tomás returned his attention to the *Penthouse* Pet of the Month.

Crossing the hall, Hoop saw that the back door was wide open, and Mitchell, the postman, was wheeling in a stack of boxes on a hand truck. Hoop opened the Shipping and Receiving door and Mitchell wheeled his cargo in. "Bunch of 'em today," Mitchell said. "Like Christmas. Keep the door open, I got more."

Left alone with the boxes, Hoop checked the labels. Simon and Schuster, Random House, Houghton Mifflin Company, Farrar Straus & Giroux, Farrar Straus & Giroux, Farrar Straus & Giroux. By the time he had found the purchase order copies in the file, Mitchell had returned with two more cartons from FSG.

"Got anything for me to pick up?" he asked.

Hoop shook his head.

"You guys aren't shipping out as much as you were when that other guy was in charge."

"That right?" Hoop asked.

"The horseshit, dogshit guy. Usually be a box or two every day for the Returns Center. I guess you guys aren't returning as many books nowadays. I guess that's a good sign."

"Retuh,turns Center? What's that?"

"You tell me," Mitch said. "It's your store, guy. I'm just a mailman. Here, you got to sign for those five boxes from Farrar whatever."

Hoop signed for the books, thanked Mitch, and went back across the hall to finish drawing himself a cup of coffee. He returned to Shipping and Receiving, set the coffee on the counter, and methodically received the shipments from Simon and Schuster, Random House, and Houghton Mifflin. Found the packing lists in the file, opened the packages and matched the packing lists against the invoices, counted the books as he stacked them on the trolley, stowed the empty cartons, and wheeled the trolley out to the big room, where he found Jeanne McBurney straightening the reference section, with help from Howard Katz. He turned the trolley over to her and said, "All yours."

"Thanks, Hoop." She gave him a smile. "How's Luce doing these days, by the way?"

"Hell if I know."

"Oh?"

"Haven't sss...heen her lately."

"Oh."

Hoop carried the invoices and packing lists to the office, where he set them on Bernice's desk. "Harry," he said.

Harry looked up from his typewriter.

"Your shipment came in. Those Gi,gi,Gillis books."

"Oh yeah?" Harry stood up from his desk and said, "Well? How do they look?"

"Haven't opened them yet."

"Well, c'mon, then. Let's go have a look at these babies!"

"Honestly," Bernice said, "you'd think it was Christmas around here."

Back in Shipping and Receiving, Hoop handed Harry the utility knife and said, "You duh,do the honors."

Harry carefully opened box number 1 of 5. He pulled out the invoice and handed it to Hoop, then reached in and lifted out a handful of hardbound books. He handed one to Hoop, who took it with reluctant fingers.

The dust jacket had a plain, typographic design, light peach display type, Caslon Italic with swash letters, reversing out of a deep forest green:

SOFT SHOUTS
poems
Jane Gillis

He turned the book over and saw the color photograph. A lock of dark red hair fell across her forehead, covering the outside corner of her left eye. She smiled at him. Forget it, she was smiling at the world. The world who loved her, for who would not love this gorgeous, smiling woman? She began to tremble in his hands.

"Hey, what's this?" Harry said. "Check out the dedication. Listen to this: 'To Francis Johnson, for his voice, and to Robin Clarke, for mine.' That's *your* name, right? Francis Johnson? Some coincidence, or...Hoop, are you okay? Hoop? Take it easy, pal. Hey. *Hoop? Don't drop the book, okay?*"

Hoop unpacked them all. Counted them: two hundred, as ordered, including the five copies Harry had carried away. He put one copy on the counter, then repacked the boxes and put them under the counter, where they would stay hidden until the week of Janie's signing.

They'd be put out for sale on Monday, the last day of July.

Shit, Hoop thought. *That's one week from today.*

He picked up the copy of *Soft Shouts* from the counter and carried it to the office.

Bernice said, "Hoop, dear, are you all right? Harry said—"

"Fuh,fine," Hoop answered. "I need to tuh,talk to Elmer a sss...hecond."

"The door's open," Elmer called from the Inner Sanctum. "Come on in, Hooperman."

Hoop walked into Elmer's office and said, "You recognized my vah,voice."

"What's up, pal?"

Hoop held up two fingers. "I need to teh,take the duh,day off."

"How come?"

"There's no wrapping anyway. No more receiving. I'll cuh,come in to...nnight, in case—"

"Hoop, what's wrong?" Elmer asked. "You're shaking."

"Cuh,cuh,cramps."

"I thought cramps only happened to women. And their employers, of course."

"And another thing," Hoop said. He held up the book. "I want to buh,buh,borrow this for the afternoon?"

"Sure, be my guest. Bring it back like new, though. Those books are costing me a fortune. I don't know what Harry's thinking."

"He's got guh,guh,good tuh,taste."

"They'd better sell."

"If they duh,don't, I'll sss...hend them to the Retuh,turns Center."

"Returns Center? What's that?" Elmer asked.

~ ~ ~

When Hoop showed up at quarter to eight that evening, Charley grinned from behind the register and shouted, "Right on! Hooperman to the rescue!"

"What?"

"The new evening shift guy, the one replacing you? He quit."

"He di,di,didn't last long."

"Never showed up. Called the store half an hour ago and said he got offered a better job at Discount Records in Menlo Park. So I'm stuck behind the fuckin' register, man. Millie won't come up from the back room." Charley darted his eyes right and left, then said in a stage whisper, "I gotta take a leak so bad I can taste it, man."

"You want me to—"

"Cover the register for fifteen minutes? Would you, Hoop, my main man?"

"Fi,fi,fi,fififteen mi,mi,m—"

"Thing is," Charley explained, "if I have to take the register till eleven, it'll be a lot easier on me if I could also spend a few minutes beforehand in the parking lot, you know what I mean. What do you say?"

Hoop shrugged and smiled. "Be buh,back by eight," he said. "I guh,gotta hot duh,date."

"You're on, man. Thanks a bunch. Take the phone off the hook, if you want."

"I'll duh,deal with it."

The phone didn't ring, and there were only two customers to ring up on the register, and so Hoop had an easy time of it, except for the passage of time, as eight o'clock got closer. His gaze kept returning to the schoolroom clock hanging over the front door. The big hand climbing. Would she come in through the front door, or did she expect him to meet her out behind the store? He wanted to hold the big hand back.

Eight o'clock.

Eight oh one. Oh two.

Where was Lucinda? Maybe out back?

Where was Charley? Maybe out back? Maybe both of them out back? Him helping her bring in the boxes of books, her helping him smoke a joint, both of them leaving Hoop stranded at the register.

Eight oh five. Ten. Fifteen. *Shit*.

At eight twenty-two, Palo Alto Police Officer Ned Reese swaggered through the front door of Maxwell's Books and approached the register. He seemed to be trying, and not trying very hard, to keep a shit-eating grin under control. He nodded.

Hoop nodded back.

Officer Reese said, "So you're in charge here?"

"Teh,teh,temporarily."

"I forget your name."

"Juh,dge...ohnson. Fuh,fuh—"

"You're a judge?" Officer Reese's grin was trying to escape.

"No. Juh,dge...ohnson is my name."

"Well, Judge Onson, looks like you are in charge here for the rest of the night. Your partner?" Officer Reese pulled a pad out of his shirt pocket and checked his notes. "Mr. Charles David? Right?"

"Yes?"

"Well, we're taking him in. Gonna book him. Just thought I'd let you know."

"Teh,teh,taking him in? Whhh—"

"Possessing and using an illegal substance. Smoking pot, I think you peaceniks like to call it. Am I getting through to you, Judge?"

Hoop nodded.

"Mr. David asked me to let you know you're in charge. He also asked me to get his purse for him. Said it's under the counter. Purse. The man carries a *purse*. Whatever. Got it there?"

Hoop looked under the counter and found the woolen Greek bag Charley David carried with him everywhere. He handed it to the officer.

"Purse. Jesus. Oh well. So anyway, you may want to phone Mr. Maxwell and let him know what's happened. He'll probably need to post bail tomorrow. Oh, and we're also taking in that colored woman." Reese checked his notes again. "Miss Baylor. Same charge. Just using, not possessing, as far as we know. We'll know more about that after we search her car. Also Mr. Maxwell may want to press charges against her. It appears she was stealing books from the back of the store. She said she wasn't stealing them, but that's how it looks. Five boxes of books right next to her vehicle. We're having the vehicle towed. And searched. We'll leave the boxes in the parking lot so you can bring them into the store. I'm sure that's what Mr. Maxwell would want."

"Where are they?"

"The books?"

"The pi,pi,people."

"They're in the back seat of our squad car. Officer Barker is keeping them company while I come in here to collect Mr. David's ID. His *purse*. Then we'll take them over to the station and book them." Officer Reese hefted the Greek bag. "Have a nice night."

"I'm cuh,cuh,coming with you. Out buh,back."

"No you're not."

"But—"

"Unless you want a free ride to the Bryant Street Station.

That what you want? Huh? You been smoking grass too, big fella? Huh?"

Hoop sat on the stool behind the register, shivering. The phone rang, and he let it ring. Customers came up to the register to pay for their purchases, and he took their money and counted their change silently. He watched a kid boost a copy of *Elephant Bangs Train* from the window display and walk it out the door, and he didn't get off the stool to stop him. Time stretched out as the minutes passed, then time snapped back. At quarter to nine, Hoop took a paper bag from the cubby beneath the register and wrote a note.

You need to call Elmer right away. The cops busted Charley and Lucinda out in the parking lot. Smoking dope, the cops say. Officers Ned Reese and Tom Barker. They took them to the police station on Bryant. They'll be in jail overnight, need bail in the a.m.

Also I need to do some work in Shipping and Receiving. Will you relieve me at the register?

He stood up from the stool and carried the note to the back of the store. He found Millie wheeling the empty trolley down the center fiction aisle, Nabokov to Steinbeck.

"Mi,mi,Millie."

She stopped and turned to scowl at him.

He handed her the note.

As she read, her expression blossomed from irritation to fury. "They *what?*"

Hoop nodded.

"Those fucking pigs!"

Hoop nodded again. "Will you cuh,call Elmer?" he asked.

"Can't you do that?" she asked. "No, I guess you can't. Oh, all right. And yes, I'll take the register. Shit. Those *assholes!"* She gave the trolley a push to nowhere, then shoved Hoop out of her way as she set off for the front of the store.

Hoop wheeled the trolley to the back hall. He pushed the EMERGENCY EXIT ONLY open and used a brick to block the door from closing.

There they were. Five cartons of books, stacked in two piles. Hoop carried the boxes into the Shipping and Receiving room, one by one. He unpacked the boxes and sorted the books on the counter, arranged by sections in the store. He racked the books onto the trolley, as many as would fit, and wheeled the trolley out into the fiction section.

He finished reshelving all the books Lucinda had brought back by ten thirty. Then he returned to Shipping and Receiving and closed the door behind him. He started with the drawers of the desk. Nothing but supplies, including the tape dispenser, so that wasn't missing after all. Then the filing cabinet, which was filled with publishers' catalogs. He checked the pine shelves that lined one wall of the room, where he had expected to find piles of books ready to wrap and ship. They were empty.

He stood on the chair, then stepped up onto the Masonite countertop for a different perspective.

There.

On top of the bookcase, where only Martin could have reached it.

Hoop climbed down off the counter. He pulled two full boxes of *Soft Shouts* from under the counter and placed them in front of the book case. He slipped out of his sandals and stepped up onto the boxes, then reached over the top of the bookcase. There. He got his fingers around it and brought it down.

He set the spiral-bound notebook on the desk, slipped back into his sandals, and placed the cartons of books back under the counter with the other three cartons. He moved the chair over to the desk and sat down and opened the ledger.

Martin's handwriting was remarkably small, fastidious, and readable.

It was a record of shipments made, date by date, package by package, weight by weight, destination by destination.

Books to mail-order customers.

Weekly returns to Penco-Pacific, Bookpeople, Raymar, L-S.

Returns of defectives and overstock to publishers' warehouses.

And—two or three each week, for the past two years—shipments to The Returns Center. No address, just the name.

He heard Millie shuffling through the back hall, then knocking on his door. "Hey, Hooperman, it's after eleven, man. Time to close up. Time to go home."

Hoop closed the shipping log and placed it in the top drawer of the desk. He silently shut the drawer and stood up.

"Cuh,coming," he said.

As he closed the Shipping and Receiving door, he asked her, "You cuh,cuh,call Elmer?"

"He'll be here at eight tomorrow morning. He wants you to meet him here."

"Qu,question."

"What?" Millie said. "Come on, man, I want to get out of here. What?"

"What's the Retuh,turns Ssss...Center?"

"I don't know what in the hell you're talking about, Hoop. I hardly ever do."

A SOFT APOLOGY

Dear Francis,
I am filled with guilt. My gain
has been your loss. My growing brought you pain.
But knowing how to speak out loud is more
addictive than I know how to ignore.
Your voice is something I was thankful for,
but now with my own voice I've learned to roar
out loud, out loud, a sound I never knew
I'd love, or love it more than I need you.
You helped me grow, and with your help I grew
from pleasing you to more. I wowed a crowd.
And that's what sucks. It sucks. It sucks out loud,
and I am so ashamed of being proud.

There's still a part of me that will remain
forever quiet and forever yours.
Your Jane

CHAPTER TEN

When Hooperman got to the store at seven forty-five Tuesday morning, on July 25, he found Elmer already there, brewing coffee in the staff kitchen. The big bear-face gave him a scrunched look, somewhere between a grimace and a grin, and said, "Good morning, Mr. Johnson." He pointed to a sack on the table. "You eaten yet? Grab yourself a bagel. Coffee's almost ready."

Hoop sat at the table, extracted a poppy-seed bagel from the bag, and waited for Elmer to put two steaming-hot mugs on the table. "Milk?" Elmer asked, his hand on the refrigerator door.

Hoop shook his head. "Buh,black. Thank you."

Elmer sat and the two men faced each other through the steam while they picked at their bagels. Elmer said, "So."

Hoop answered, "Lucinda Beh,Baylor duh,doesn't smoke duh,duh...marijuana."

Elmer waved a hand as if to shoo away an irrelevant fly. "I've already talked to Mort Sanderson. You remember Mort?

Lieutenant? Okay. So I'll tell you what I know at this point, and then you tell me what you know. Okay?"

"Okuk—"

"So. Two police officers witnessed Charley David smoking a joint in the parking lot behind the store. That's against the law. They arrested them, because smoking marijuana is against the law. Lucinda was keeping company with him while he was breaking the law. That's also grounds for arrest."

"Buh,but—" *I never smoke that stuff,* she had said. *Does bad things to me.*

"Hush. I'll give you a turn. The cops were within their rights. They were allowed to arrest her on suspicion of using an illegal substance, given the circumstances. Maybe that's not fair, but it's legal. However, at the police station she was questioned and appeared not to be under the influence of anything illegal. Her car was searched for illegal substances, and they found nothing. So all marijuana charges against her were dropped."

"Thank Guh,God. Ssss...ho where is she?"

"They kept her overnight. No, let me speak. There was another charge. She has been kept overnight on suspicion of stealing books from my store. A lot of books. Five cartons of books. *From my store.*"

Hoop's hand shook and he spilled hot coffee on his fingers. He slammed his mug down and said, "Nnnnot tuh,tuh,true!"

Elmer looked down at the table and shook his head. When he raised his face to Hoop, he was wearing a transparently false imitation of a humble smile. "Hooperman Johnson, are you calling me a liar? Because Mort Sanderson read the arrest report to me. Are you calling my friend Mort a liar? The report, filed by Officer Ned Reese, said that five cartons of books, new books, were stacked next to Lucinda Baylor's car. According to the report, Lucinda told Officer Reese that the cartons, and the books in the cartons, all came from Max-well's Books. Now. Are you calling Ned Reese a liar? Or are you calling Lucinda Baylor a liar?"

Hoop kept his mouth shut.

Elmer checked his watch and said, "You and I have an appointment at the Bryant Street station at nine o'clock. Mort Sanderson is expecting me to press charges. Based on what I know at this point, I plan to do just that. It would be good if I knew what you know. Besides, Mort Sanderson's going to ask you some questions about this. You might have an easier time talking to just me."

Hoop kept his mouth shut. *Just don't tell Elmer about this,* she had written. *I'm trusting you.*

"Hoop, listen to me. Let's work together here. If you can convince me that Lucinda wasn't stealing books from my store, I'll drop all charges as soon as we get to the police station. Now. What about that?"

Lieutenant Mort Sanderson ushered Elmer and Hooper-man into his overstuffed office, unfolded a couple of metal chairs, and invited them to sit down. Then he took a seat behind his desk, which looked like a monument to anarchy: books, papers, writing tools, a full ashtray, half-filled coffee mugs, a wide sprinkling of paper clips and rubber bands, yellow pads, manila folders, an intercom, a telephone, and a Rolodex. As for the lieutenant himself, he looked as if he had already put in a full day's work. His shirt was rumpled, his sleeves were rolled up, and his tie was at half mast. He hadn't shaved that morning.

He lit a Lucky Strike and shook out the match. "Elmer, you got me up early this morning," he said. "I ought to file charges." He balanced the cigarette on the lip of his ashtray.

Elmer chuckled. "Actually, pal, I want you to drop charges.

Lucinda Baylor was not stealing books."

The lieutenant combed his hair with his fingers, leaned back in his chair, and said, "You're sure about that? You're the one who asked us to keep her overnight. So now you're sure you want her released?"

"Quite certain," Elmer answered. "I owe her an apology. Right, Hoop?"

"We all do," Hoop said, looking from Sanderson to Elmer and back again. "Apuh,puh,pup...ology."

Sanderson nodded, took a drag from his Lucky, and said, "Okay." He pressed a button on his intercom and told somebody, "We need a charge dismissal form on the Baylor woman. Release her."

The machine said, "Okay."

"I'd like to speak with Lucinda before she leaves the station," Elmer said.

Hoop shuddered. *I'm trusting you.*

Sanderson told the intercom, "Bring her to my office after she's signed for her personal effects."

"Okay."

"Now then," Elmer said. "Shall we drop those ridiculous charges against Charles David, too?"

Mort Sanderson shook his head. "Charles David isn't here anymore. He was transferred down to San Jose at six a.m. He's now a guest at Santa Clara County Corrections. He'll be arraigned tomorrow. You can post bail then if you want to."

Elmer gave his friend Mort the knotted brow look. "I want you to get him out of that hole. I mean it."

"You know I can't do that, Elmer. The kid was smoking dope. They caught him red-handed. Shit, he didn't even try to hide it. The officers were in their squad car, for Christ's sake, and he blew smoke at the windshield. It's like he wanted to get caught. He was breaking the law, period. End of story."

"Maybe he thinks it's a stupid law," Elmer said.

"Of course it's a stupid law, Elmer. You know it, I know it, I expect Hoop here knows it, but it's the law."

"There was once a time, Morton Sanderson, when the sanctity of the law was not as important to you as the difference between right and wrong."

"Calm down, Elmer. If you're talking about my conscientious objection to war, I always worked within the system. And so did you."

"You were a cuh,cuh,conscientious objeh,dge...ector?" Hoop asked.

Lieutenant Sanderson nodded.

Elmer said, "Mort is one of the Old Guard. He worked with Harry Thornton and me on a Civilian Public Service farm project in North Dakota during the early forties. The Old Guard still gets together once a month and plot against the military-industrial complex. You'll be there next Tuesday, right, Mort?"

"Chopsticks for Peace," Mort said. "I'll be there."

"We probably won't see Martin," Elmer said. "The bastard quit on me."

"No shit?"

"Well, you know Martin. There's plenty of shit, but none of it makes sense. I'm afraid it appears Martin's the one who's been ripping me off."

The door to the office opened, and Lucinda walked in, slowly, as if into a den of hungry lions. Her face was a ticking time bomb. She found a place to stand next to Sanderson's desk where she could look each of the three men in the face. She looked at the police lieutenant and shook her head. She slowly turned her face to Elmer's and stared at him with contempt. She shook her head again. Then she fixed her glare on Hooperman Johnson.

"I never want to see you again."

"Luce—"

"I told you not to tell Elmer."

Elmer said, "Sweetheart, he was doing you a favor."

She took her time answering. She squeezed her eyes tight, took a deep breath, opened her eyes and let tears leak down over her round, brown cheeks and said, "Well, thank you all very much." To the lieutenant she said, "For the hospitality in your charming bed-and-breakfast that smelled like piss and vomit, I'll return the favor by never setting foot in your lily-white city again." To Elmer she said, "Thank you, Elmer, for asking these kind gentlemen to put me up overnight. I'll re-pay you by never setting foot in your phony store again." And to Hoop Johnson: "Thanks for nothin', man. Little fucker. *Snitch!*"

She slapped her hands to her weeping face and bolted from the office.

On their short walk back to the store, Hoop asked Elmer, "Dih,did you mi,mean what you sss...haid to the lieu-teh,tenant? About Muh,muh,Mmartin? Sti,stealing buh, books?"

Elmer sighed. "I don't know, kiddo. Maybe, maybe not. If Martin's been ripping me off, good news/bad news, right? He got away with it, okay, bad news. But he's gone now and I can stop worrying. If it was Martin."

"What if he comes buh,back?"

"We'll see. I don't think he'll come back. He's a mess, you know. The bastards fucked with his brains."

"You tuh,told me. What's guh,going to happen with Chuh,chuh,Charley?"

"I'll post bail, and I'll get him a good lawyer. Shit. You'd think he'd be a bit more discreet. New rule. No smoking in the parking lot. Grounds for dismissal. No exceptions. Jesus Christ, Hoop, don't ever try to run a small business with a staff full of counter-culture bozos."

"Aren't you cuh,countercuh,cuh—"

"I'm not a bozo. Oh, by the way, can you work the evening shift tonight? I still haven't found anybody to replace Lucinda, and now with Charley out, that leaves just Millie. How about it?"

They reached the front door of the store before Hoop answered. "I guh,guess so," he said. *Shit. Another evening with Millie.*

So it was that Hooperman was perched on the stool behind the register on Tuesday evening, alone in the front while Millie wheeled the trolley around the fiction aisles in the back room. Fortunately Tuesday evenings were slow, with only a handful of customers, and they were browsers who didn't ask for information. Even the telephone cooperated with him, while he sat behind the register, trying to forget two women by reading an issue of *The Saturday Review of Literature.*

He read the entire magazine, right up to the classified ads. Halfway down the second column, under the heading "Book Search," he saw a boxed ad:

REPUTABLE BOOK SCOUT
recent first editions, our specialty
send want list to The Returns Center
Box 35922, Mountain View CA 94035

Returns Center? Mountain View? Lucinda lives in Mountain View, he thought. Oh, Jesus. He shut his eyes and shook his head.

"Good evening, Judge Onson."

Hoop opened his eyes and found himself looking up at the grinning face of Officer Ned Reese. *Dumb fuckhead.* "Cuh,can I help you?"

The cop tilted his head back a bit to allow him to stare down at Hoop, sighting him along the line of his nose. "I believe I can help myself," he said. "Guess I caught you napping, huh?"

Hoop stood up from the stool, so that the two tall men stood eye to eye. Hoop saw the other cop, Tommy Barker, duck into the aisle between Languages and Travel, a couple of magazines under his arm.

"You guh,guys shh...ure you don't need any help?"

Ned Reese's grin stretched over his nicotine-stained teeth. "I believe we can help ourselves, Judge. That okay with you? If we help ourselves?"

"I guh,guess. Looking for sss...homething special?"

"Just doing our job, sir. We're patrolling. Making sure you don't get robbed. Or bombed. Serving and protecting, that's our line." The cop pulled off a mock salute, then sauntered down between Political Science and Sociology, toward the back of the store.

Hoop was stuck at his post behind the register. He doubted that he would have followed the cops back through the labyrinth of aisles in any case. He found the Palo Alto Police Force more than a little difficult to have a conversation with.

He wrote the Returns Center postal address on a slip of paper, folded the slip, and pocketed it, then carried *The Saturday Review* back to the magazine rack facing the front door.

He knew the next customer to come into the store, too, and this one was even more difficult for him to talk to. "Hello, Mr. Johnson," said the white-haired faculty member. He wore his western academic clothes: sportcoat and fresh-pressed jeans.

Hoop nodded and said, "Sir."

"The beard looks good on you. I didn't know you were working at Maxwell's. We haven't seen you on the campus in a long time. Mary and I were sorry to hear about you and your wife."

Hoop shrugged. "Cuh,can't win 'em all."

"I suppose you can't. But as I understood it, the reason you turned down the fellowship was that you wanted to go with Jane to Ann Arbor."

"Yup."

"But you didn't go with her, so you could have accepted the grant after all. Seems a shame you didn't do that."

"Shh...hame," Hoop repeated. Deflated, he sat back on the stool.

"Frank, why don't you apply again?" the professor gently urged. "We're full for this coming year, but after that, I have no doubt—"

"I duh,don't write anymore," Hoop croaked. "I'm ssss... horry!"

The professor's blue eyes widened, then narrowed to a squint. "I'm sorry too, Frank. My God. You have such a unique voice."

Hoop laughed nervously. "Sss...ho I've been tuh,told."

"You're a writer, my friend," his former mentor told him. "You can't escape that. You'll write again. When you finish that novel, let me know. I plan to see it in print."

With that, the professor hitched up his jeans, turned, and ambled away through the aisles toward the back.

"You assholes!" Millie's voice carried through the store. Fortunately there were few customers to offend. Unfortunately, the only customers who ought to have been ashamed burst out laughing. They stopped at the front door and Tommy Barker called back, "You must be mistaken, Miss. We're officers of the law."

Millie stormed into the front room. "I don't give a flying fuck who you are, you're ripping off magazines."

Ned Reese turned to Hoop and said, "Didn't you tell me we could help ourselves?"

"I duh,didn't sss...hay you could shhh...hoplift."

Both policemen held out empty hands.

Millie appealed to Hoop. "They tucked magazines under their belts, behind their jackets! Skin magazines! Do something, Hoop! Frisk them, for Christ's sake!"

"I'd advise against that, Judge," Reese said.

Barker added, "Just doing our routine surveillance, sir. You can tell Mr. Maxwell we observed no theft tonight, and no threat of a bomb."

The snickering cops left the store.

Millie threw up her hands. "Shit, Hoop!"

"Excuse me?" said the professor as he emerged from the aisle. "I overheard that exchange, and I also witnessed the pilfering in the back room. They helped each other stuff magazines under their belts behind their backs." He pulled a wallet out of his back pocket as he walked over to the register. He laid a business card on the counter in front of Hoop and said, "If you need a witness, call me. I'll be happy to make a statement about what I saw. And Frank? I want to hear from you about that other matter, okay?"

Hoop could feel the red-hot blush throbbing in his face. He nodded.

The professor nodded back, smiled, turned, and left the store.

"Lot of good that'll do," Millie said. "Some old geezer accusing the Palo Alto police? Who's going to believe him?"

"He's known for bih,being honest," Hoop told her. "Well known."

Millie walked to the counter and picked up the card. "Wallace Stegner? You know Wallace *Stegner?*"

"Ssss...hort of. You know him?"

"Are you kidding?" Millie put her hand on a front-table stack of *Angle of Repose.* "Besides, he has a whole shelf in the back room, right above Steinbeck. How come you know him?"

"Long ss...tory. You gotta cuh,call Elmer."

"That'll be your call, man. You're the one who knows the witness."

The commotion had brought a few curious customers to the front of the store, where they browsed as if they weren't paying attention to Hoop, but Hoop knew better. He took one terrified look at the phone, then shook his head at Millie. "I ceh,ceh—"

"Want to call him from the office phone?" she asked.

"Locked."

She dug a key out of her jeans pocket and handed it to him.

"You guh,got a ki,ki,key?"

"Give it back when you're done. I'll handle the register. Make it fast. I still have a ton of books to shelve."

"Elmer's phuh,phone number?"

"Use the Rolodex on Bernice's desk. God, Hoop, you're so helpless."

Hoop let himself into the office, turned on the light, closed the door, sat down at Bernice's desk, and twirled the Rolodex until he found Maxwell, Elmer. He dialed.

"Elmer Maxwell."

"Elmer. This is Hoop."

"Is this the Hooperman who doesn't talk on the telephone? Congratulations—"

"Shhh...ut up, Elmer, this is hard enough as it is."

"Sorry. Okay. Your move. Take a deep breath and go slow. What's up, pal?"

So Hooperman took his time and stumbled through the whole story.

"God, that's great!" Elmer said when he'd heard it all. "I knew you'd be a fine bookstore cop. Was I right, or was I right?"

"I duh,didn't fuh,frisk them," Hoop said.

"I'm glad you didn't try," Elmer said. "You'd be calling from the police station. You did the right thing. Stegner? Hoop, how do you know Wally Stegner? Never mind. God, this is great. I can't wait to call Mort Sanderson. In fact, I'll call him tonight."

"What's he guh,going to duh,do?"

"I'm not above a little extortion," Elmer answered. Hoop could hear the glee in his voice. "I predict Charley David will be out of jail, all charges dropped. He'll be back in the store in time for his shift tomorrow night. Good work, lad. Now get back on the register and sell some more books."

After hanging up, Hoop spun the Rolodex to West, Martin. He took the piece of paper out of his pocket and wrote down Martin's address in San Jose, right under the Mountain View PO Box address of The Returns Center.

Returns Center. He spun the Rolodex to the R's, but there was no card for the The Returns Center.

He looked up Lucinda. There she was: 3129 Easy Street. Mountain View.

Not Lucinda. Who else? Martin, probably, but he lived in San Jose.

Millie?

Millie Larkin. No address, just a phone number.

Now what? Go through the whole staff and find out who else lived in Mountain View?

The intercom buzzed. "Come on, Hoop. Hurry up, man. I need a little help up here."

Hoop walked into the inner sanctum and tucked Wallace Stegner's business card behind the dial on Elmer's telephone. Then he came out and headed for the door out of the office. Just before switching off the light, he turned back and returned to Elmer's office for another look at a sheet of paper he'd seen on the desk. On Maxwell's Books letterhead, it was a letter dated that day, July 25, 1972. Addressed to:

Ret urns Depart ment
Simon & Schust er
1230 Avenue of t he Americas
New York, NY 10020

Dear Sirs,

Please send ret urns aut horizat ion and labels (2) for t he following overst ock books. Invoice numbers list ed below:

"Hurry up, Hoop, Goddammit!"

HOOPERMAN VISITS HIS MOTHER

In the December after Janie left him, as Christmas was coming on strong, with carols piped throughout the Stanford Shopping Center and false holly draped all around the Town and Country Village, Hoop finally decided it was time to go to Shaker Heights and visit his mother. She'd been begging him for months to "come home." She had offered to send him a plane ticket. "Anytime," she had pleaded. "You're always welcome."

But he didn't take a plane. He decided to surprise her instead. He took the Greyhound from Palo Alto to San Francisco, then caught another bus east through the winter, with stops in Reno, Salt Lake City, Cheyenne, Omaha, and Chicago. The trip took three nights and two days, and ended in downtown Cleveland in time for breakfast on Christmas Eve. Hoop carried his bag two blocks through a blizzard to the Terminal Tower, where he ate eggs and bacon, then caught the next Rapid Transit train out to Shaker Heights. A local bus dropped him right in front of his mother's house.

She opened the door. *"Yes? What can I...Frank? Frank! My goodness! You have a beard! Come in, come inside, out of that storm! Oh Frankie, let me give you a hug! Thank God you've come home! Just leave your bag here in the hall for now. Why didn't you tell me you were coming?"*

He hugged his mother and followed her into the living room. They sat and smiled at each other. *"Can I get you any-thing? Cup of coffee? Are you hungry?"*

"I had buh,breakfast downtuh,town."

"It's so good to see you. I've missed you so, you know that."

Frank nodded. *"No Cuh,Christmas decorations,"* *he noted.*

"I didn't know you were coming."

"Still Cuh,Christmas."

"Well, somehow it didn't feel like Christmas this year, not without you and Janie. I mean, well, not without you." *Her face turned red.*

"And Juh,dge...Janie. I agree," *he told her.*

"You must miss her so."

He tried to shrug, but all he could manage was a twitch.

"I know what," *his mother said.* *"Let's decorate the house today! In time for Christmas."*

"We don't have to."

"But I want to! Don't you?"

"Okay."

"We can't go outside in this horrible weather anyway, so we might as well decorate. Oh, this is going to be such fun? Isn't it?"

"I guh,guess."

It took all morning. Then they settled at the kitchen table and had lunch, Campbell's chicken noodle soup and toasted cheese sandwiches, which they washed down with beer.

"We should throw a party," Clara said. "Have all your friends over? How would you like that? Maybe even New Year's Eve."

Frank didn't expect to be in Shaker Heights that long, but he was careful not to bring that up just yet. "I expect they all have other puh,plans."

"Well, then, let's make it the following Saturday. We could have a cocktail party. Hmm?"

Frank set down his soup spoon, "Mother, I duh,don't have any fuh,friends left in Shhh...haker Heights."

"Of course you—"

"Never really had any fuh,friends here but Juh,dge... anie."

Clara turned to the kitchen window. "This weather is just ghastly," she said.

He cleared his throat and told her:

"Freeze, freeze, thou bitter sky
That dost not bite so nigh
As benefits forgot:
Though thou the waters warp
Thy sting is not so sharp
As friend remembered not."

After lunch, Frank went to the room where he had slept as a child. He lay down on the bed and took a nap. One beer after a three-day bus trip was enough to make him sleep like a child in the overheated house of his childhood.

He awoke after dark, went into the bathroom, and showered. He emerged from his room wearing clean clothes and the best Christmas smile he could muster.

The house was brightly lit with color. Since there was no tree, they had gathered ornaments—red, blue, green, silver, and gold balls—into bowls and placed them on the coffee table, the stereo speakers, the dining room table, bookshelves, the top of the piano. Every tabletop had a lit candle or two, placed on diamond-shaped mirrors. Fuzzy reindeer paraded across the mantel. Mr. & Mrs. Claus dolls sat together at one end of the sofa. An antique crèche had its yearly place of honor on a table in the front hall.

There in the living room stood his mother, dressed in a lustrous green dress, with a sprig of plastic holly pinned to her graying hair. She grinned, rubbed her hands together, and announced, "Goodie. You're just in time for cocktail hour."

"Cah,cocktails."

"Why don't you lay a nice fire, and I'll go mix us a drink. What'll you have? Martini? Old Fashioned?"

"Whatever you're having."

"Let's have Old Fashioneds. Some whiskey for a stormy night."

She left the room and Frank turned to the fireplace. He laid kindling first, then oak logs across the andirons, turned on the gas jet, and lit the fire with a long match. Fwoom. When he was sure the fire had taken hold of the logs, he cut off the gas, stood back, and admired the fire's warmth and warm light until his mother re-entered the room.

She placed a tray on the coffee table. Two golden brown cocktails, and a bowl of mixed nuts. "Isn't this Christmassy?" she asked. "Oh, Frankie, thank you for coming home in time for Christmas."

They clinked glasses, smiled, sipped, and smiled again.

She said, "I expect you have all sorts of plans, but I thought I should mention that Harold Gillis wants to offer you a job."

"Juh,dge,Janie's fuff, fuff, fuff—"

"Janie's father, yes. He'd like you to work for his com-

pany. And I thought—"

"Why?"

"I don't know. He's always admired you." She drank. She gobbled a few nuts and sipped again.

Frank shook his head.

She took a long swallow from her drink. "Well, I suppose he feels a bit responsible for what happened. Although it's not his fault, but you know. He's pretty steamed at Janie, if you want to know the truth. Harold and Alice both. Well, we all are, frankly."

"Juh,dge,Janie di,did what she had to do."

"Anyway, Harold thinks it's only fair to offer you a job. He wants to."

Frank laughed, as if this were funny. "Doing what?" he asked.

"Well, writing, I suppose. He knows what a good writer you are. You'd be perfect for his firm. Public relations. Press releases, news stories. Harold's a big Cleveland booster, and...well, I think you should talk to him about all this. He thinks so highly of you. You know that."

"I don't think I could write puh,press releases."

They drank in silence for a few minutes.

Clara rattled her ice cubes and said, "Well, it was just a thought. How about another drink?"

During the second drink, she said, "Well, you have to do something, Frank. That's important. I mean the important thing is to be doing something. Right?"

"I do things."

"The Cleveland area has so many opportunities. You'd be surprised."

"Mother, this is a vvvisit."

"I know that, sweetheart, but—"

"*My home is in Puh,Palo Alto.*"

Her mouth was a thin, straight line. "*Isn't that a place of bitter memories? Honestly, Frankie—*"

"*My work is there.*"

"*What work?*"

"*Writing. I'm a writer, Mother. What I duh,duh,do.*"

"*Your novel? Are you working on your novel again?*"

"*No. The novel dah,died.*"

"*When Janie left?*"

"*Befuh,fore that.*" It was when Janie started to speak out loud. Started seeing Robin Clarke. "*I just dec...ided that I duh,don't write fuh,fuh,fiction.*"

"*You could, though. You were good! Are good. You were given that fellowship. The chapter I read, the one that got published in the* Paris Review? *Gosh, that was so good, Frank. I don't know why...well then, for heaven's sake, what do you write?*"

"*Literary cuh,criticism,*" Frank answered. "*I guh,guess you could cuh,call it.*"

"*And you can make a living doing that?*"

"*Puh,pays pretty guh,good.*"

"*Where is this getting published?*" She crunched a pecan and washed it down.

Hooperman took his time. He passed a hand over his face and tugged on his beard. Finally, without looking her in the eye, he said, "*I'm a guh,guh,ghostwriter, Mom.*"

Clara Johnson drained her glass, chewed on her cherry, and then said, "*I don't understand. Tell me what that means. Ghostwriter?*"

He took a deep breath and let it out. "*I write tuh,term peh,papers. Mostly about puh,poetry. Fuh,F rost, Hart Cuh,Crane, Milton...When I get buh,back I'll be writing a muh,muh,masters thesis about World War One poets: Owen,*"

Suss...ass...oon, Guh,Graves—"

"You're writing students' papers, and they pay you."

"Guh,good money."

"Isn't that illegal?"

"Not exactly."

"But it's wrong!" She reached into the bowl with a shaky hand and scooped up a few nuts. She popped them into her mouth and repeated as she chewed, "It's wrong, Frank."

"It's a living," he said. "Sss...homething I enjoy duh,doing. Where I duh,don't have to tuh,talk to puh,people. Would you rather have me buh,bus teh,tables? What do you want me to duh,do, Mother? Besides work for Harold Gi,gi,Gillis, I mean?"

Clara shook her head. "I want you to throw two more logs on the fire. I want you to go out in the kitchen and pre-heat the oven to four hundred; we're having chicken pot pies. And I want you to bring me another drink."

"I don't know how to make an Old Fuff—"

"Bourbon on the rocks will be just fine, thank you very much." She handed him her glass, with a weak imitation of a smile.

When he returned to the living room, he found her stand-ing in front of the picture window, as if she were looking out onto the snow-blanketed back yard. But when he stood be-side her, all they could see was their own reflections in the gaily decorated living room.

"Merry Christmas, darling," Clara Johnson said.

"Listen to that wind," Frank replied. He handed her the drink.

She said, "Blow, blow thou winter wind. Thou art not so unkind as man's ingratitude." She sat down on the couch and placed the drink carefully on her coaster. She buried her face in her hands and her shoulders began to shake.

"Muh,muh,Mother?"

She looked up at him. Tears were flowing over her cheeks. She said, "You know, Frank, I was terribly sad to lose Janie. I loved her so much. But you know what? You know what, Frankie? It hurts a whole hell of a lot more to be losing you."

CHAPTER ELEVEN

Wo wo, wo wo, wo wo wa wo-wo
bm ch, bm ch, bm ch, bum ch
Wo wo, wo wo, wo wo wa wo-wo
Do you know the way to...

SAN JOSE
FIRST ST
NEXT EXIT

Hooperman took the off-ramp, leaving the Bayshore Freeway and entering a city he barely knew. He drove past the city center, approaching San Jose State University, but before he reached the campus he turned left on Jackson for a few blocks, then right on Ninth. He cruised Ninth slowly until he found the number he was looking for, then parked his rust-colored Bug next to the curb.

He took a long look. The lawn was brown and dry, but two loquat trees were heavy with fruit. The house was a 1920s-style bungalow, off-white stucco with a red tile roof. Twin bougainvillea climbed like red and purple monsters on either side of the round-topped wooden door. Bird of paradise plants stood like proud orange and blue storks along the front of the house. Curtains were drawn across the windows on both sides.

Hoop took a deep breath, blew it out through trembling lips, and got out of the car. He opened up the trunk in the front of the VW and retrieved the spiral-bound ledger, which he tucked under his left arm. He sauntered up the cement walkway, stood on the front doorstep, bit his lip, pressed the doorbell, and listened to the chimes of Big Ben.

To his vast relief, there was no response from within. He breathed and shrugged. *Tried, at least,* he thought. *Maybe this wasn't such a good idea anyway.* Just to be thorough, he rang the chimes again before turning around, and this time, to his chagrin, he heard the thump of heavy approaching foot-steps. *In for it now.*

"Horseshit. Heard you the first time." The door swung open and there stood the tall ogre, the crazy man, the book thief, the book scout. He wore the same gray tee shirt, the same oily jeans, and the same snarl. The bald head was sprouting a five-o'clock shadow, and a coffee stain ran like a dry creek through the brambly gray beard, from the right side of his mouth down past his chin.

"Pig shit. Horseshit pigshit cowshit. What in the horseshit pigshit dogshit do you want?" He nodded his head four times, shook it once, and fixed Hoop with a glare.

Hoop said, "I have your juh,dge...ob now." He held out the shipping log. "You left this. Want it buh,back?"

"Horseshit." Nod, nod, twitch. He took the log and said, "Horseshit. Thanks. Anything else?"

"Ceh,can I ask you a qu,question? Ssssss...some qu...

questions?"

"Horseshit. Dogshit. Horseshit dogshit catshit batshit. What?"

"May I cuh,come in?"

The look on Martin West's face gradually shifted from snarl to smile. His teeth were stained and crooked, and Hoop had no idea what the smile was about. The smile of a spider who feels the jiggle of prey in his web? The huge man swung wide the door and swept a path through the air with the shipping log. "Come the horseshit on in."

The furniture in Martin's living room was bulky and rough, just like Martin, but comfortable. They sat in armchairs, facing each other across a crude coffee table, and Martin said, "Do you want a cup of horseshit. Cup of pigshit. Dogshit. Cup of cowshit." He shook his head and tried again. "*Coffee*. Want some coffee?"

"No thanks. I had some already."

Martin nodded and nodded again. "So. What?" He rested his leathery bare feet on the table and mumbled, "Horseshit."

I'm really in for it now. "Is this the Returns seh,Center, Muh,Martin?"

Martin balled up both fists and pounded the arms of his chair. *"What?"*

"The Returns Ssss...center? Are you the Retuh,turns—"

"Horseshit! You got to be horseshit. You got to be horseshit. Joking. You got to be *horseshit,* joking."

"So you're not the Returns Suss...Well then, who is?"

Martin answered with a long and involved shrug. He twitched, nodded, twitched again.

"But you were suss...hending out all those puh,packages to the Returns Suss...Center. They're in that log, Muh, muh,muh—"

"Horseshit pigshit cowshit dogshit."

"They are. I—"

"Of course they are. I wrote that. Horseshit."

"Well, why did you—"

Martin grinned. "I vass yust following orrders. In the horseshit."

"Whose orders?"

"Shit if I know. Dogshit. Millie gave me the stacks of returns. With the labels. Horseshit pigshit." Nod. "She left them on my shelves every night, and I wrapped them up, individually, and shipped them horseshit pigshit the next morning. Catshit." Twitch.

"Did you know that Mi,mi,Millie accuh,cused you of guh,groping her? The night before you qu,quit the sss...tore?"

"Bullshit!"

"Muh,Martin, I've never heard you sss...hay buh,bullshit before."

"Horseshit pigshit cowshit dogshit. That's bullshit! I never groped her. Horseshit, never groped anybody, ever." The twitch in his face took over his upper body, traveling south to his shoulders and out through his arms to his massive hands, which flopped on the arms of his chair and turned into granite fists. "Horseshit pigshit cowshit dogshit, batshit catshit ratshit. *Shit!*"

"I bih,bih,believe you. Weren't even there that night, right? In the sss...tore?"

"Horseshit dogshit. I was there. Shit."

"What fuh,for? You leave at fah,five. Left, I mean."

"Wanted to talk to Millie. Horseshit." Nod.

"So? What fuh,fuh,fuh—"

"Not to grope her in the horseshit. Dogshit."

"Sss...ho?"

"Tell her it was stupid. Tell her no more returns to the Returns Center. Didn't make any horseshit sense. Return books the day after I receive them? What kind of horseshit horseshit is that? Book comes in on a Thursday, brand new title, horseshit, same title goes out to the Returns Center the next day in the horseshit. One or two copies. Make sense to you? Horseshit pigshit dogshit, dogshit pigshit." The snarl was back. And the twitch. "So I told her, no more horseshit bogus Returns Center bullshit, or I'd talk to Elmer about it. And that's when Millie went apeshit."

"Cuh,can you puh,prove this? That the sss...hame buh,books were, that you, I mean the sss...hame buh,books—"

"Horseshit. Stay here. Horseshit." Martin rose in sections from his armchair and strode out of the living room. When he returned a couple of minutes later, he was carrying five ledger books identical to the one lying on the coffee table. He laid these five on top of the new one in a precise stack.

"Goddamn horseshit shipping logs going back five years. A horseshit record of every horseshit cowshit shipment I made while I worked for that dogshit pigshit store. Elmer horseshit Maxwell's store. Up till this year I even listed the books I sent and where in the horseshit I sent them. Kept lists of the books I sent, including horseshit lists of the titles I sent to the Returns Center, and the horseshit dates. Lot of them new titles. Brand new. Horseshit pigshit. Shit. Take a look." Martin sat back down in his chair, reached out, and opened the top book on the file at random. He pointed at the page. "June 19, 1969. Horseshit. Returns Center. Horseshit. Look: *The French Lieutenant's Woman*. Two copies. Brand new horseshit. Brand new book, horseshit dogshit pigshit. Came in the day before." Nod, nod. Nod.

"You remember that? How cuh,can you buh,be shhh... sure?"

"You think because I talk weird, horseshit pigshit and like that, I'm automatically stupid? Horseshit pigshit?" Nodded, shook his head, nodded again. Shook his head again. "Huh?"

Hoop laughed out loud.

"Funny? You think it's horseshit? You think it's *funny?*"

"Fuh,funny? Shhhh...hit, yes! Fuh,fuh,fucking hilarious!"

Martin snarled for a minute, then let his mouth grow into a wide-open grin. "Ratshit batshit catshit gnatshit!" he said, and laughed. "Couple of horseshit crazies, huh? You and me? Horseshit!"

"Duh,dumbells!" But when the laughter died down, Hoop asked, "How do we puh,prove that these went out the duh,day after they fuh,first cuh,came into the sss...tore?"

"Find the horseshit. Find the horseshit. Find the Little Brown invoice. Bernice's filing cabinet. Horseshit."

"How do I guh,get into the office and ssss...hearch the fuh,files when nobody's there?"

"Horseshit." Martin offered a hopeless shrug and shook his head. "Dogshit."

"I could guh,go in there at night."

"Horseshit. Locked up."

"Mi,millie might let me in. She's guh,got a ki,key."

"Horseshit."

"But Mi,mi,Millie's the one we're tuh,trying to cuh,catch. Right?"

"Who's 'we'? Horseshit. I don't work there anymore."

"Muh,muh,Martin, why'd you qui,qu,quit? Mi,Millie went apeshit? What's that mi,mi,mean?"

"Horseshit dogshit pigshit. Told me to shut up or she'd have me fired. Horseshit! Nobody can fire me. It's my horseshit. My job, and they can't take that away from me. Horseshit cowshit pigshit dogshit. Fuck them. So I horseshit quit. I get disability. Live on that. Dogshit." Twitch. Twitch.

"Do you know where Mi,mi,Millie lives?"

"I'm going to guess horseshit. Horseshit, Mountain View.

Why do you want to know?"

"Thought I'd puh,pay her a cuh,cuh,call. But I don't know her address. And the only aduh,dress I have for the Returns Suss...Center is a puh,puh,post office buh,box." He pulled a piece of paper out of his shirt pocket and read, "Box 35922, Mountain View, California 94035."

Martin shrugged. "So go to the horseshit. Go to the horseshit. The post office. Go to the Mountain View main post office. Horseshit. Go first thing tomorrow morning. And wait."

That evening Charley David was back behind the register, just as Elmer had predicted. Grinning, he told Hoop, "Yeah, man. All charges dropped. Thanks to you, my man. Elmer told me about those pigs, how you nailed them. You saved my ass, man. You and Elmer."

"Sss...ho how does it fi,feel to be a fuh,free man?"

"Good!" Charley said. "Well, mostly. I'm not quite as free as I was. But that's cool. Yeah, that's cool. You know?"

"What's cuh,cool?"

"Elmer got me out of jail and got me out of trouble. But I had to promise him not to smoke dope on the job anymore, which is a bit of a downer. But whatever. So from now on I'll just do a number on my way to work and another number on my way home after the store closes. But you know, I mean, you know. Eight hours is a long time between numbers."

"Sss...ho how was juh,dge...ail?

"Not bad. Not a bad place to visit, I mean. Wouldn't want to live there."

"Fuh,food shh...hitty?"

"No, man. Check it out, rice and beans. Brown bread. Tap water." Charley did a *namaste* with his hands. "Right out of the macrobiotic cookbook."

Howard Katz walked out of the Political Science aisle, over

to the bullpen, and leapt to the counter by the register. He knocked over a penny cup and methodically pushed four pennies, one at a time, over the edge with his paw.

Hoop said, "Hey, Howard." He put his hand on Howard's shoulders and rubbed it down his back. As he got closer to the tail end, Howard turned away, lowered his shoulders, raised his rump, held his tail straight up, and saluted Hoop with his anus.

"That reminds me," Charley said. "Lucinda?"

"Yes?"

"She thinks you're the cat's ass, man. She told me so on Monday night while we were sitting there waiting to get booked. They kept us in this hot smelly room for over an hour. All she talked about was you, Hoop. Hoop this, Hoop that. What'll Hoop think of me now? Is Hoop going to hate me? He's going to think I'm a thief, she says. Man. Lucinda is *not* a thief, Hoop."

"I know that."

Charlie said, "You need to tell her. Sounds like she's way into you, man. You ought to give her a call, you know? You know her number?"

"You muh,mean a phuh,phone call?"

"Shit. Yeah, I hear you. Phones and all. Listen, take off a few minutes, go across the street to your apartment. Call from there."

"No phuh,phone in my apuh,partment. It's okay." Hoop scratched his chin through his beard. "I'll cuh,call her from the office."

"Wish you could, man." Charley took over petting Howard Katz. "The office is locked."

"I'll buh,borrow Mi,mi,mi,Millie's ki,key."

"Millie? She doesn't have a key. Nobody does. Elmer's too paranoid, you know that."

Hoop nodded. "Yeah. I guh,guess you're right. Buh, bathroom, okay?"

"Right on, man."

Hoop walked around to the front of the counter and picked up the four pennies. He put them in the penny cup and turned toward the back of the store. He didn't stop at the men's room, but walked on through the center room and into the back room, where he found Millie pushing the trolley laden with mass market paperbacks up the Science Fiction aisle from Brian Aldiss to Roger Zelazny.

"Mi,mi,Millie."

Millie halted the trolley, turned to Hoop, and raised her eyebrows, which Hoop knew to be shorthand for Yes? How can I help you? or What the hell do you want?

"Cuh,can I buh,borrow your ki,ki,ki,key?"

"Key?"

"To the office?"

"I don't have a key to the office. Nobody does but Elmer and Bernice and Harry."

"You had a kuh,key Mmmonday night."

"Yeah, well I found that. In the kitchen. Somebody must have left it there by mistake. Bernice, probably, she's so absent-minded sometimes."

"You guh,gave it buh,buh—"

"I left it on her desk last night. Jesus. What is this, Hoop? What are you, some kind of Perry fucking Mason?"

"Haven't bi,been many reteh,teh,turns to shi,ship out sss... hince I tuh,took over Muh,Martin's juh,dge...ob."

"So? It's seasonal."

"None at all to the Retuh,turns Ssss...Center. Sss...hince I took over."

"Shut up, Hoop. Would you please just shut up?"

"You don't want me to tuh,talk about the Retuh,turns—"

"I don't want you to talk about anything, man. You know, you're not all that much fun to listen to, if you really want to know."

Hooperman smiled and nodded, and didn't say *See you tomorrow, honeybunch.*

HOOPERMAN THE BUSBOY

"*Excuse me, but aren't you Francis Johnson?*" *The tall, bald, kindly-looking gentleman wore a dark suit. With a smile and a shrug he held out his hand. "I'm Wilbur Hall."*

"*Di,Dean of Acadeh,demic Affuh,fairs,*" *Hooperman said as he shook hands.*

"*That is correct. Would you be good enough to sit down with me for a few minutes? I'd like to chat with you. We could go over there in the corner, where we'll have a little privacy.*"

"*I'm suppuh,posed to be working.*"

"*I wouldn't worry about that,*" *the dean told him. "I know the food services director. Very good friend of mine. Please.*" *He led the way.*

Hoop set his bussing tub on one of the empty tables, slung his damp rag over his shoulder, and followed Dean Hall to the far corner of one of the back rooms. He pulled the accordion wall shut behind him. It was four in the afternoon and the student union was nearly empty. He knew he wouldn't be missed for a few minutes.

He sat down opposite the dean and waited.

"We expected you to be earning your master's in English this year, Mr. Johnson. You were awarded a fellowship in the Creative Writing Program."

Hoop nodded.

"Instead, I find you bussing tables and washing dishes for Tresidder Union, a job that's usually filled by scholarship students."

Nodded again.

"Well, okay, never mind that. But this job pays minimum wage. Dollar twenty-five an hour. Is that enough for you to live on?"

"I duh,don't need much."

"You must have some other source of income. Am I right?"

Hoop shook his head.

"Mr. Johnson, do you know Ned Eubanks?"

Hoop nodded.

"How do you know Ned Eubanks?"

"English Depuh,partment."

"You're a man of few words, aren't you, Francis Johnson."

"Sss...ho they teh,teh,tell me."

"Well, I'll get to the point. Mr. Eubanks tells me you also earn money on the side, as a research assistant, helping students with their term papers, and so on. Is that true, sir?"

Hoop paused and moved his head in a way that was neither a nod nor a shake, or both a nod and a shake. "Used to," he admitted. "Duh,don't anymore."

"You quit? Why was that?"

Hoop squinted at the Dean of Academic Affairs and told him, "I realized it was wrong."

Wilbur Hall nodded. "You came to a good decision. Every

Stanford student is bound by our Honor Code, as you know."

"I wasn't a sss...tuh,student at the tuh,time."

Dean Hall's face reddened. "I'm disappointed in you, Mr. Johnson. Student or not, I—"

"I'm disapuh,pointed in me tuh,too, sir."

"Well, never mind. The point is, the kids you wrote those papers for were students. And each of them violated the Honor Code, even if you were exempt because of a technicality. So the point is, I want you to tell me the names of the students for whom you wrote papers that they turned in as their own work. Will you do that for me?"

Hoop shook his head.

"Why not?" Sweat beaded on the dean's brow.

"Cuh,client cuh,confidentiality."

Dean Hall drew a white handkerchief from his breast pocket and wiped his face. "It doesn't upset you that Ned Eubanks told me what you had done?"

"You can ask him, I guh,guess. He knows the names of the others." Hoop pushed back from the table. "I think I should geh,get buh,back to work."

"Wait, please, Mr. Johnson. I'm not quite finished with you."

"Yes?"

"I don't think it's right that you're taking a job in this student union that ought to belong to a scholarship student, do you? Do you think that's fair?"

"Well—"

"There may not be any rule against hiring outsiders, but as I said, I know the head of food services, and the point is, I want you off this campus by this time tomorrow, and I want you to stay off this campus. Have I made myself clear?"

Hoop stood up, smiled at Dean Wilbur Hall, bowed, and said, "Guh,glad to obuh,blige."

Hooperman knew why Ned Eubanks had spilled the beans. It was because Hoop had reneged on his agreement to write Eubanks's master's thesis on the poets of World War One. Hoop found out through the grapevine—he still had friends in the English Department, including his advisor, Tom Moser—that Eubanks had told on Hoop's four other clients, all of whom were expelled and exiled from academia. Eubanks left Stanford voluntarily and transferred to the University of Southern California. His father, Lester Eubanks, who had made a killing in Southern California real estate following World War II, pledged a million dollars to the Stanford Fund and another half-million to U.S.C.

By this time Hoop Johnson was much in demand on the Midpeninsula. He bussed tables up and down El Camino Real, from the Bib 'n' Tucker to Rudolfo's, from Dinah's Shack to the original Round Table. He bussed on Castro Street in Mountain View, home of the best ethnic restaurants between San Jose and San Francisco. He ended up moving about the eateries of Palo Alto: Bennington's Cafeteria, the Seven Seas Chinese, Ramona's.

He knew how to wipe down a table, how to stack a bus tray, how to keep his mouth shut for hours on end, and how to run the dishwashers when the dishwashers didn't show up.

Finally, in the spring of 1972, Hooperman took a giant step up in his career in the food business and became a pizza chef at 'At's Amore Pizza Pie Palace on University Avenue. Minimum wage was now $1.60.

That same spring, on the Stanford University Campus, Ned Eubanks, Ph.D. became an associate professor of English, a shoo-in on the fast track to tenure.

CHAPTER TWELVE

Hooperman was at the steel and glass front door when the main branch of the Mountain View post office opened at nine a.m., Thursday, July 27. He had found a place to leave the Bug, three blocks away, free parking all day. He walked into the building, set his work down at the writing table in the front corner of the lobby, then wandered around until he located Box 35922. He bent down and peeked through the glass window, and saw mail waiting to be picked up.

Bingo.

And perfect: Box 35922 was wedged in the corner, in view of Hoop's post at the writing table, but far enough away so that she probably wouldn't see him spying on her. She'd have to stoop down, take her time, then stand up and turn around, and there he'd be. Smile on his face.

"Fancy seeing you here," he'd say.

"Hooperman?" she'd exclaim, all flustered, trembling. "What in the fuck are you doing here?"

"My job," he'd answer, smooth as you please. "I'm a bookstore cop, remember? And you, Miss Millie Larkin, are under arrest."

Just like that!

Hoop sat down, opened the Eaton's box, and arranged the pile of paper on his corner of the writing table.

"What the hell are you talking about, Hoop? I never know what the hell you're talking about. Because you can't talk for shit, Hoop. You know? You sound like a busted roto-tiller, you creep."

And Hoop would reply, calm as you please, "I'm talking about the Returns Center, honeybunch. The Returns Center, don't you know."

"What Returns Center?" she'd ask, of course, like she always does, pretending she never heard of the Returns Center, like she always does.

And Hoop would smile pleasantly down into her frightened face and say, "Could I please have a look at that handful of mail you have there?"

"No fucking way," she'd say, or maybe "Mail? Male chauvinist pig is more like it, asshole," and she'd start to walk around him, but she'd be shaking so hard she'd drop an envelope or two from her pile of mail, and Hoop would be all over it.

He would read aloud: "'The Returns Center. P.O. Box 35922, Mountain View, California 94035,' Miss Larkin. Your address, Millie. Your business address!"

Gotcha!

Ten o'clock. Time to admit that he might have to wait all day before she came into the post office. Time to admit she might not even come that day.

Time to admit that Hoop had to take a leak, and he could use a cup of coffee, and sometime that day he'd have to get some lunch and eat it outside the building, because there was a sign on the table: NO FOOD OR DRINK. What if Millie came in to collect her mail while he was out of the building?

Well, at least he'd know. He'd look through the glass window of Box 35922, and if the box was empty, he'd get the rest of the day off. But he'd be back tomorrow. Tomorrow and tomorrow and tomorrow, watching for creeps in this petty place, day after day. Until she shows up. As long as it takes, to catch a thief.

Meanwhile, what Hoop really had to admit was that he really, really, really had to take a leak.

Leave his papers on the table? Sure. It was the only copy of his novel in progress, but what difference did that make?

Twelve forty-five, and she still hadn't shown up. But the mail was still in the box, and Millie didn't have to be at the store till five o'clock, same as Hoop.

Hoop returned to the job at hand: reading through *Parts of Speech*, pages 1-175, as far as he'd written before he stopped writing the novel, in the spring of 1964. This was the first time he'd looked at the manuscript in eight years.

It was hard getting past the dedication page.

Then, as he forged ahead, he realized that Janie was on every page of the novel. Every page, in one ghostly way or another, and that made every page just as difficult to read as the dedication page.

Worst of all, from the distance of eight years he was able to see that the novel was not bad. Good, even, maybe. Worth continuing. Worth opening the wounds for. It needed tinkering, but what it really needed was some sort of desire to finish telling this tale, if only to find out how it would end. What would happen? Did Hoop even want to know? Or did he already know?

Meanwhile, time for lunch. He left the post office, this time with the novel back in the box and tucked under his arm. He walked to the deli on the next block and bought a salami sandwich and a Coke, which he carried back to the granite steps in front of the P.O. He ate his lunch, dumped his trash, and returned to his post at the writing table. He checked Box 35922: still stuffed.

He sat down and returned to his tinkering. He was up to page 94. Every page was a pain in the ass.

He soldiered on. Page after page, looking up after every other sentence, hoping to be interrupted by Millie Larkin and her furtive scowl.

By three o'clock Hoop was aware that his chances of seeing Millie that day were diminishing, and so was his desire to catch a thief.

So was his admiration for the tear-jerking, award-winning, brilliant and tedious novel he was plowing through page after dreary, dazzling page. Did he really care what happened to these characters whose dialogue might have been written by Mel Blanc?

Did he really want to be a real writer or did he want to be a real person?

Did he want to write self-pitying crap? Bile syrup?

He drummed his pencil on the table.

He looked up.

P.O. Box 35922.

A crouching figure, with a clutch of Jiffy Bags under one arm, was opening the box and pulling out a handful of mail. Then sorting through the envelopes, smiling.

The suspect carried the bundle of letters and the handful of packages to the window. Hoop understood now. The thief was mailing Elmer Maxwell's books out to his own customers, loyal patrons of The Returns Center, Reputable Book Scout, Recent First Editions, Our Specialty.

When the thief was finished at the window, he slapped his incoming mail against his hand and strode out of the building, while Hoop breathed an apology to Millie Larkin, wherever she was. *I should have known,* he thought. *The typewriter.*

He rose from the writing table and walked over to the pay phone in the corner. He dropped in a dime and listened for the *plong,* then dialed the number.

Bill Harper answered. "Maxwell's Books, may I help you?"

"Hi, Bi,Bill. Cuh,could I ssss...peak to Elmer?"

"Hold on, Hoop."

Elmer came on the phone a few seconds later, and after a full minute of false starts and sputter, Hoop got his boss to agree to meet him for breakfast the next morning at eight o'clock, Easton's Coffce Shop on University Avenue.

He walked back to the table, put the unfinished *Parts of Speech* into its box, tucked the box under his arm, and dropped it in the trash can on his way out of the post office.

Hooperman Johnson wasn't meant to be a writer, and he knew it. He wanted to work for a living, not write about it. Bus boy, whatever. As for now, he was a bookstore cop, and a loyal employee of Maxwell's Books of Palo Alto.

He was also a man who had no idea what to do next, but that didn't bother him much. Instead of writing about life, he'd muster the courage to live through it, if only to find out what would happen.

And the hell with bus boy.

Francis Hooperman Johnson had fallen for the book business.

Since he was already in Mountain View, and he didn't have

to show up for work until five, he pointed his VW with his heart and within five minutes parked it in front of 3129 Easy Street.

She opened the door and he stood on the threshold, taking in the familiar aroma of pasta sauce. "Hi, Luce," he said, grinning like a fool who didn't mind being a fool. "How you duh,duh,doing?"

"Hoop, dollbaby!" She wiped her hands off on her apron, threw her arms around him, gave him a quick hug, then pushed him back a pace. "What brings you here? I returned those damn books, every one."

"I fuh,found out who was sss...tealing buhbuh buh, books."

"I told you, Hoop, I returned—"

"Yeah. Wait. Not you." Then he told her.

"You're shitting me."

"I shhh...hit you not."

"I don't believe it. I mean, I believe *you,* but I just can't believe it. So what will you do?"

"I'll tuh,talk to Elmer about it. Tomuh,morrow muh, morning. Want to come with me?"

"Breakfast with Elmer? I don't think so."

"He owes you an apuh,pology. You shuh,shush—"

"Forget it, Hoop," she said. Then she laid a hand on his shoulder. "It's nice to see you again, baby. It was nice of you to drop by." They still hadn't moved any farther into the apartment than the doorway.

"How late do you sss...tay up? I could duh,drop by again after work?"

She turned away. "I have a date tonight, Hoop." It was almost a whisper.

Hoop nodded. "Puh,puh,pasta," he said.

She said, "It's all I know how to cook."

"Sss...herious?"

She turned back to him and shook her head.

It took all the courage he had, but he had nothing to lose. "Then how about we spuh,spend the weekend toguh,gether? Guh,go somewhere, maybe?"

"I don't think I'm ready for that, Hoop. You either."

"Mi,mi,mi,mi—?"

"You. Your ex-wife's coming to town, remember? When is that, again?"

"Next Thursday."

"A week from right now. Don't tell me that's not on your mind."

"It's nnn—"

"It is too," she snapped. "Let's wait till that's all over and see how you feel. I'm not going to risk falling for you again, my friend. Not till I know I'm your first and only choice."

The door closed in his face before he could think up a reply, let alone say whatever words he might have come up with.

Later that afternoon, while Charley manned the bullpen up front, Hoop mustered his courage and strolled back to the fiction section, where he found Millie on her knees, attacking the bottom shelves with a feather duster.

"Millie."

She looked up and answered by not answering.

"I, um, um, um, I want to, I want to—"

"Aw for God's sake, Hooperman, just spit it out. I'm too busy for this."

Hoop could feel the blood surging to his face, could almost hear the grinding of his jaw. All his life people had told him to "just spit it out," and this was the first time he'd ever told them how much that helped him articulate.

"If I could sssssss...pititout, dud,dud,dud,dudoncha think I

fuh,fuh,fucking would?"

Millie shook her head. "What did you want to tell me, man?"

"I'm ssss...horry," he told her. "That's what."

She stood up slowly, in stages. She slapped the feather duster against her thigh and said, "As usual, I have no idea what you're talking about, but whatever it is, you're wel-come." She shook her head. "Sorry for what?"

"For thinking you were the Retuh,turns Center."

She turned a furious red and said, "I swear to God, man, if you mention that Returns Center one more time, I'll scream bloody murder. You're as bad as Martin West."

"Muh,Martin didn't tuh,try to guh,grope you," he told her. "Di,did he."

"He accused me of ripping off the store," Millie said. "Him and you both, seems like."

"I know you di,didn't rip off the sss...tore, Millie. I know that now."

"Okay then. So get out of my face. I have work to do."

"He dih,didn't guh,grope you," he told her again. "Muh, Mmartin."

Millie set the feather duster on a shelf full of Louis Lamour. She crossed her arms over her chest and said, "You weren't there. He scared the shit out of me. He blocked the door so I couldn't get out of that creepy Shipping and Receiv-ing room. You don't know, Hoop. You don't know what it's like to be threatened by a man. You've never been raped."

"You're right. But I duh,don't believe Muh,Martin was guh,guh—"

"Okay, all right, okay. I overreacted. Give me a break, man. Martin's a scary man."

"He's a juh,dge...entle man, Millie."

"No such thing, Hoop. Men are bigger than women, and

Martin's bigger than most men. He could have beat me up. It all comes down to that, doesn't it."

"Not if pih,people listen to each other."

Millie's eyes opened wide. "Listen? Listen to Martin West? Are you kidding?"

"We all sss...peak dih,different llanguages, Millie," Hoop said.

She nodded. "I wasn't really going to tell Elmer anything, you know. I wasn't going to have Martin fired. I admit I'm not sorry he quit. But I swear to God, Hoop, I know nothing whatsoever about this Returns Center you and Martin keep going on and on about. And if you keep badgering me about that I know how to make life difficult for you."

Hoop smiled. "My life's already a little dih,difficult right now. Tuh,truce?"

Millie shrugged, even smiled a little bit. "Whatever," she said.

HOOPERMAN FINDS A HOME

On a gray day in March 1972, Hooperman parked in the lot behind Maxwell's Books, walked around the block, and crossed University Avenue. Happy to see the sign still in the window of 'At's Amore Pizza Palace, he walked into the dark, savory restaurant and strode up to the bar.

The man behind the bar, a gray-haired gent with a thin mustache and a greasy apron, grinned and said, "So what can I do for you on this fine day, my good friend?"

"Apuh,puh,partment for rent?" Hoop answered. "Ssss... hihn says inqu,quire within."

The man held his hand out across the bar and said, "Hey, there. My name's Vince Amore. And you?"

"Hoop Juh,dge...ohnson." Hoop shook Mr. Amore's hand.

"The place is upstairs. Come on, I'll show you. You're gonna love it."

"Now?"

"No time like the present, like the man said. Come on." Vince Amore took off his apron and shouted to a woman

who was wiping pizza crusts and scraps off a lacquered table in the back. "Back in a minute, Doris. You're in charge."

Doris saluted and returned to her chore. There were no customers in the Palace at three in the afternoon.

Hoop followed Mr. Amore out the front door and into an alley beside the building. Mr. Amore unlocked a door and led Hoop up a dark stairway, then down a dark hallway. At the end of the hall he opened another door, and said, "Voilà. Home sweet home. Fully furnished. And it's all yours for seventy-five dollars a month, utilities included."

Hoop walked into the one-room apartment and looked around. Linoleum floor, double bed, dresser, table and four chairs, armchair and a pole lamp, kitchen area with sink, half-size fridge, hot plate, and a cupboard. He opened the closet door: three wire hangers on a wooden rod. He checked out the bathroom. The shower smelled okay, the toilet flushed, and the sink worked, even if it had a stain of mineral deposit from the tap to the drain.

He walked to the studio's only window and gazed out at the view of University Avenue. "I'll tuh,take it."

"Rent in advance," Mr. Amore told him. "First and last. And a thirty-dollar cleaning deposit."

Hoop walked across the room and sat down at the table. He pulled out his wallet and counted out nine twenties.

Amore scooped up the money. "A man of means, I see. Hoop, tell me something. You're not a student, are you? See, thing is, I don't like renting to students. Parties and stuff, you know what I'm talking about."

"I'm not a sss...tudent." Hoop stood up and returned to the view, the best feature of an otherwise shabby one-room flat.

"I hope you're in for the long haul, Hoop," the landlord said. "I've had a hell of a time renting this place, I don't mind telling you. And full disclosure and all that: the restaurant

downstairs can get kind of noisy nights. Especially week-ends. Okay?"

"No puh,problem."

"You seem to like this apartment."

Hoop smiled at downtown Palo Alto and gazed at Max-well's Books, directly across the street. "Location, location, locuh,cuh,cation," he said.

"Work nearby, do you?"

"Not really."

"You got a job, Hoop? I mean you do work for a living, right? You'll be able to come up with the rent? See, the way you're dressed...."

"I'm a dih,dishwasher. Keh,Ken's House of Peh,Pancakes. Menlo Park."

"Food service. I like that. Too bad you're not a cook. I had to fire my pizza chef last night. So now I'm looking for—"

"I could do that," Hoop said, thinking: location, location, location....

"Uh, the reason I fired my chef? He talked too much. I don't like a cook who talks all the time. How are you with that?"

Hoop smiled, shook Mr. Amore's hand, and said, "Not a puh,problem, Vince. No puh,problem whatsoever."

CHAPTER THIRTEEN

At 7:15 p.m. on Tuesday, August 1, Hooperman pulled into the parking lot at Ming's Chinese Cuisine on Embarcadero Avenue, east of the Bayshore Freeway. He parked his rusty Bug next to Elmer's gleaming Jag, got out, took a deep breath to settle his nerves, and walked to the front entrance, carrying a manila envelope. Inside he told the hostess, "I'm with Chah,Chopsticks for Pi,Peace."

She smiled and led him to a small private dining room at the back of the restaurant.

Elmer clinked his water glass as Hoop walked into the room, and when the mumbles and chatter stopped he said, "Blindfolds all in place, panel? Mystery Guest, will you sign in, please?"

They all turned toward him, and Hoop felt drilled by their wondering eyes. They were all there, the Old Guard: Elmer Maxwell, Jack Davis, Pete Blanchard, Harry Thornton, Mort Sanderson, and even Martin West, wearing his scowl and his Levi jacket. Bernice Rostov, the bookkeeper, was also at the large round table. She smiled warmly and said, "Hoop, what a surprise!"

Hoop said, "Were you a cah,contientious objeh,dge...ector, Buh,buh—"

"My husband was," she answered.

"He was the bravest of us all, Ari Rostov," Elmer said, and his fellow objectors nodded. "Hoop, have a seat. There's an extra place between Jack and Pete. And help yourself to some food. There's plenty left."

Hoop sat down, laying the manila envelope in his lap. He picked up the package of chopsticks that lay across his plate and slid them out of their paper wrapper, then rolled them between his hands as he waited for somebody to break the awkward silence.

At long last, Pete said, "What the hell, Elmer? We're inviting guests now? Outsiders? No offense, Hoop, but we're supposed to be building a society without war, and I fail to see how—"

"Oh for God's sake," Jack muttered, plowing into Pete's tirade. "You and your damn protocol. Why not mix up our plays a bit? This group could use a kick in the pants, if you ask me."

"If we asked you, we'd have no structure at all."

"Damn right. War is all about defending structure."

"Damn *wrong*. Are you saying war is in the Social Contract?"

Bernice said, "Children, hush."

Mort grinned, Martin rolled his eyes heavenward, and Harry said, "Spin that lazy Susan, would ya, Elmer? I want some more of that Kung Pao chicken. While there's any left."

Elmer tapped his glass with his knife again. "People, now that our friend Hooperman Johnson is here, I'd like to call the meeting to order."

Hoop glanced around the table and saw that again all eyes were on him. He drummed his plate gently with a chopstick.

Pete cleared his throat. "Are you sure about this, Elmer? I mean, personally, I like Hoop, but isn't this setting a dangerous precedent? And what can he contribute to what we're trying to accomplish?"

Elmer smiled. "Perhaps we could let Hoop answer that."

Hoop took a deep breath and said, "It's about a buh,bookstore puh,problem."

Harry, the buyer, held up his hand. "Now wait a minute. I like Hoop, too. I think we all do. But we have an agreement, Elmer. No bookstore talk at Chopsticks for Peace. Talk about protocol, talk about precedents."

"Sh...rinkage," Hoop went on.

Jack, the anarchist, said, "Elmer, are you ever going to let go of that issue? Christamighty, *every* business has shrinkage. It's just a form of entropy. We have to live with it. The whole universe is shrinking."

"Expanding," Pete said.

"Shrinking. As in going down the drain."

Mort said, "I want to hear what our guest has to say."

"I'm with Harry," Pete said. "We shouldn't be talking about store business. We have more important problems to fix."

Mort shook his head. "Maybe Hoop has something worth hearing. Maybe if we fix the shrinkage problem in Maxwell's Books, that will be the first small step on the long, long road to world peace."

"Oh, give me a break," Bernice sang, "where the buffalo roam...."

Elmer clinked his glass again. "Shrinkage..." he began.

"Jesus," Harry grumbled. "Have to work in that store forty, maybe fifty hours a week, you'd think we could have one evening a month off."

"You took off early last Thursday afternoon," Elmer pointed out.

"Yeah, and I'm always the first one in the store on weekday mornings. I work my ass off for that store, Elmer. For you, my old friend, so if I have a personal errand to run every now and then, I leave early. So?"

Elmer glared at Harry, then swept his gaze around the table, then brought it back to Hooperman. "So, Hoop. What were *you* doing last Thursday afternoon?"

Hoop lined his chopsticks up parallel to each other, pointing to Pete, the man on his left. "I spent the deh,day, whole deh,day, at the puh,puh,post office in Muh,muh,Mountain View. Main buh,branch."

"Doing what?" Elmer asked.

"Abuh,bandoning my nnovel, mostly."

"And what did you see there, in the Mountain View post office?"

Pete coughed and whined, "What the hell, Elmer? Are you some kind of Perry Mason? What are you accusing Hoop—"

"Hush," said Bernice. "Let Hoop talk."

"Since he does it so well," Jack inserted, then grinned. "Joke," he explained. "No offense, Hoop."

Hoop shrugged, said, "None taken," and swiveled his plate around to the right, so that the chopsticks pointed at Jack.

Elmer said, "Go on, please."

"Sss...hee, I was watching Buh,Box 35922."

"Why?"

"The Retuh,turns Sss...Center. That's the buh,box number."

"Returns Center?" Jack said. "Never heard of it."

Pete said, "Me neither."

Bernice said, "You mean you two actually agree about

that?"

"What the hell are you talking about, Johnson?" Harry asked. "So you went on some wild goose chase?"

Hoop took his time. He swiveled his plate slowly until the chopsticks were pointing across the table, at two o'clock. He looked down at the chopsticks, then sent his gaze slowly advancing across the table, over the lazy Susan, and on and up until he was staring into Harry's frowning face.

"You're the guh,guh,goose, Harry."

Harry sputtered and slapped his napkin on the table. "Sorry, pal, but I don't follow. Hey, can we get some more of that garlic snow-pea mushroom dish? Looks like Mort and Bernice ate the whole—"

"Go on, Hoop," Elmer said. "Are you telling us Harry Thornton is also known as the Returns Center?"

"I saw him pi,picking up his meh,mail."

"So the hell what, for Christ's sake? So I picked up my mail. Shit."

"So Box 35922 is your box, Harry?" Elmer asked.

"As a matter of fact it is. And yes, I picked up my mail on Thursday afternoon. Now can we just—"

"And Hoop, you say Box 35922 is also the box of the Returns Center, which nobody seems to have heard of?"

Hoop looked around the table at the wide-eyed and wary Old Guard. He brought his gaze back to Harry, who shifted in his chair and broke eye contact. Hoop pulled the manila envelope up from his lap and drew from it the current issue of the *Saturday Review of Literature*. He opened it to the classified ads in the back and read aloud the passage he had highlighted in yellow: "'Reputable book scout, recent first editions our specialty, send want list to The Returns Center, Box 35922, Mountain View, California 94035.'"

He looked up to watch the Old Guard shifting their attention to Harry, whose scowl had turned purple. "Okay, so I have another business, a cottage industry, a part-time *hobby*, for Christ's sake. So what? So I make a few bucks as a book scout. Why shouldn't I? I can't be expected to live on the salary Elmer Maxwell pays me. Shit. What is your problem, Elmer? Huh?"

Mort Sanderson said, "So you sell books through the mail, is that it?"

Harry nodded. "Simple mail-order business. On the up-and-up, officer."

"And where do you get these books you sell through the mail?"

"Other dealers, same as any book scout. Christ, Mort, what's with the third degree?"

Elmer said, "Hoop, where do *you* suppose Harry gets his stock?"

Hoop took a deep breath and answered, "Meh,Maxwell's Books."

Elmer looked around the table, silently acknowledging the questioning looks. He nodded slowly, sadly.

Harry Thornton laughed a little too loudly. "Come *on,* people. Elmer? Are you going to take the word of this freak of nature?" He looked around at his fellow conscientious objectors, as if grasping for some solidarity. "I mean *really!*"

"Go on, Hooperman," Elmer said. "What else you got?"

"I sss...haw Harry at the sss...tore at sss...hix this muh, morning."

"I always get to the store early! I already told you that. So I can get some fucking work done."

Bernice said, "Harry, I conscientiously object to your language."

Hoop said, "I saw you in the puh,parking lot at ss...hix, puh,putting buh,books in the trrrunk of your cuh,car."

"That's a damn lie."

"Hoop?"

"You used to puh,pull buh,books early in the muh,morning and puh,put them on the shh...elf for Mah,Martin to wrap up and meh,mail out, to the Returns Suss...Center. Now that Martin's guh,gone, you just sss...tick them in your cuh,car."

Elmer said, "So in other words, Harry, you weren't just ripping off books, you were shipping them to Mountain View on *my postage meter?* Using *my Jiffy Bags?* Harry, are you *nuts?"*

Harry raised his eyebrows, shook his head, sighed, and said, "This is so ridiculous. It's all a bunch of...I mean, for Christ's sake...why should I even bother to answer all these questions? This kid's a *child,* Elmer. You and I go way back."

Elmer said, "We do indeed. What else, Hoop?"

"I ss...haw a receipt from something called "R.C. Buh,Book Dealer" for a buh,book that was mi,missing from the sss... tore," Hoop said. "The receipt was tuh,typed on Sss...hinclair Lewis's Underwood. Ssss...paces after ti,ti,ti,tees."

"So I used the store typewriter. Big fucking deal. Who are you trying to be, anyway? Nancy Drew or somebody? Doesn't mean I stole the book, whatever it was. It probably sold, is all. Any books I sold, I got from another dealer, like I said. Happens all the time. Elmer, I beg of you, can we just drop this?"

Elmer looked at Hoop. Hoop pulled another sheet of paper out of the envelope. "Duh,duplicate puh,packing list from Farrar Sssss...traus. For those new Gi,gi,gi,Giillis books." He passed the sheet to his left, and Pete passed it on to Elmer. "We received two hundred caah,copies. I checked them in. Two hundred."

"So? They'll sell," Harry said. "If they don't they're returnable."

"We haven't ssss...tarted ssss...helling them yet."

"So?"

"As of now there are sss...heventeen cuh,copies mi,mi,missing."

"So what you're saying is somebody stole those books."

"I'm saying *you* stole those buh,buh,books."

Harry looked at his friends, one by one. The only one who didn't return his glare was Martin, who had returned to his dinner and was eating Kung Pao chicken sloppily with a fork. Harry ended up staring into Elmer's pained face. "So, old friend," he said, "what are we going to do?"

"You tell me, Harry. What are *you* going to do?"

"Everybody on the staff takes home books. You know that, don't you?"

"I don't want to hear excuses. I want you to apologize to me and to everybody at this table, especially Hoop Johnson, who is not a child, not a freak of nature, and *not* a liar. Apologize to us all, and hand me your resignation tomorrow morning, and we will part as friends. Do that, and I won't press charges. You and I go way back, Harry. All the way back to the CPS farm in North Dakota, where we worked side-by-side with Mort and Ari. We stood together then, pissing against the tide of war, and that's the way I want to remember our friendship."

Harry nodded. He rose from the table and said, "Elmer, I... I owe everyone in that store an apology. If you call a staff meeting for Sunday morning, I'll be there to say I'm sorry." He twitched, as if trying and failing to shrug. "Hooperman, thank you for bringing me in. I'm sorry I said those insensitive, inaccurate things about you." He held out his hands and smiled shakily as he looked around at the Old Guard. "Comrades, I don't dare ask you to forgive or understand what I did. I'm sorry for raising such a shitstorm this evening, and I'm glad it's over. All of it. Elmer, you'll have my resignation on your desk tomorrow morning. Typed on Sinclair's Underwood."

Harry used his napkin to wipe away the tears that were streaming down his cheeks, then dropped it across his empty plate and walked with slumped shoulders out of the dining room.

After a silence that lasted long enough to seep into the carpet, Pete Blanchard said, "Harry didn't pay for his share of the dinner."

Jack Davis said, "Just shut up."

"I was just saying."

"Just shut up."

Elmer said, "Well, Martin, it was certainly good of you to join us tonight, like old times, although you haven't said a word all evening. I'm hoping I can persuade you to come back to work at the store. We need you in the Shipping and Receiving room, now that Hoop's going to be the new buyer."

"*What?*" Hoop said.

Martin West said, "Horseshit."

Elmer said, "Thank you, Martin. I'll take that as a yes."

HOW HOOPERMAN
BECAME A BOOKSTORE COP

Almost every afternoon during the spring and early sum-
mer of 1972, Hooperman Johnson, the late-shift pizza chef at
'At's Amore, spent a couple of hours before work browsing
the shelves of Maxwell's Books across the street. By the arri-
val of summer, he was noddingly acquainted with the stock
of the store, and he knew the poetry shelves by heart. More
and more, as that spring went on, he spent the hour between
three and four up in the front of the store, where he could
glimpse the smile of the evening clerk who came on at three,
and where he could hear her sassy talk and raucous laugh
until he had to cross the street to his own job, which started
at four.

By the arrival of summer, Hoop knew enough about him-
self to recognize that the reason he showed up at the store
almost every day was no longer to read the titles of the
spines on the shelves, no longer to pet the store cat, no

longer to laugh with the members of the Maxwell's staff, but to be in the same building with Lucinda Baylor. She was the reason that whenever the Maxwell's evening shift ordered a pizza, he not only cooked it with extra ingredients, he delivered the pizza himself. He also knew enough about himself to keep his distance and limit his conversations. A crush is one thing, but one broken heart was enough for one lifetime.

But when the sign appeared in the Maxwell's front window in early July, Hoop was tempted. He saw it, more than literally, as a sign. He would have snapped at the chance to work in Maxwell's Books, even if there were no Lucinda Baylor. And there was.

So on Monday, July 10, two days after the sign went up, he sauntered across University Avenue and walked into the store grinning.

"Hey, it's Hooperman!" she said from behind the front counter. "Haven't seen you here since yesterday."

"The deh,deh,day's young yet," Hoop said. "How you dud, how you dud, how you duh,duh,dud...ooing, Luce?"

"Day's young yet. So far so good. You?"

"That ssssss...hign in the window. You guh,guh,guh,guys got a juh,dge...ob for sss hale?"

Lucinda shook her head. "Yes, but you wouldn't want it."

"Are you ki,ki,ki,kidding?"

Hoop thought: you have no idea how much I want this job.

"Elmer doesn't want to hire a clerk," she explained. "He wants a policeman. A pig."

And Hoop thought: Whatever. It's a cloven hoof in the door.

CHAPTER FOURTEEN

Wednesday morning, August 2, the day after the Chopsticks for Peace meeting at Ming's Chinese Cuisine, Hooperman showed up at the bookstore at nine o'clock to meet with Elmer in the inner sanctum.

Elmer stood up and reached his right hand across the desk. Hoop shook the hand but shook his head, too. "Elmer, I'm not the meh,man for this juh,dg...ob."

Elmer sat back down and put his elbows on the desk, his fingertips together. "Sit down, Hoop," he said.

Hoop knew it wouldn't be quick or easy, but he was resolved. He knew how this meeting would end, even if he also knew how persuasive Elmer could be.

Elmer handed Hoop a sheet of paper:

Dear Elmer,

I'm sorry. I resign. I'd like t o kill myself, but I'm nonviolent .

I'm sorry. I hope you'll find it in your heart t o forgive me.

Love,
Harry

"I need a buyer, Hoop. I want to put you to work, and in spite of what Harry said last night, the job pays pretty well. You're too valuable to stick back in Shipping and Receiving. And frankly, you talk too slowly to be a good clerk. These are the seventies, kiddo, and customers are getting impatient. No, pal, I'm drafting you for buyer. And I need you to start right away."

"I'm not a guh,good ch...oice. For buh,buyer. I meh,mean it, Elmer."

"I think I should be the judge of that," Elmer said. "I'm a fairly good judge of character, even if I did trust Harry Thornton when I knew enough not to. But that's another story. Hoop, I'm going to ask you ten questions, and I want you to answer them as honestly as you can. Are you an honest man?"

Hoop nodded. "Yes. I think so."

"Good. That was the first question. Do you work hard?"

"I tuh,try."

"Punctual? Get things done on time?"

Hoop nodded.

"Good. That's three. Do you like books?"

"Shhh...ure, but—"

"Are you familiar with the stock in this store?"

"Ssss...hort of."

"The answer is yes. You know the stock in this store better than anybody else on the staff. Everybody says so, and I take their word for it. I assume you know what's selling, and what's not selling. What do we do about books that don't sell?"

"Retuh,turn them."

"Even if we like them?"

Hoop thought a moment. "Retuh,turn them. Except in the Puh,poetry Sss...hection."

Elmer chuckled. "Okay, I'll give you that one. What about books no longer eligible for returns?"

"Sss...hale table. Duh,dollar a book. And we should have a remeh,mainder table tuh,too."

"You're getting into this, aren't you, Hoop? What do you think about sidelines, things like posters, greeting cards, book bags, paperweights, stuff like that?"

"Maybe. Why not?"

"Okay, Hoop. How do you feel about shrinkage?"

"Juh,dge...esus, Elmer!" Hoop started to rise from his chair.

Elmer laughed. "Siddown, kiddo! That was a joke. It didn't count."

Hoop fell back onto his chair and gave Elmer the fisheye.

"Okay," the boss said. "Here's your last question. Next month we're going to receive a shipment from Simon and Schuster containing a new book, a big expensive hardback titled *The Joy of Sex*. There's been a lot of prepublication buzz on this one. People are up in arms, because this book talks frankly about doing it. With pictures. Pictures of people doing it. Harry ordered five copies, and he wanted to keep it under the counter, available only on request. How many copies would you have ordered?"

"Seventy-fuh,five to ss...tart with, and ssss...tack 'em up high on the tuh,tuh,tuh,table."

Elmer smiled. It was a softer smile than Hoop had ever seen on Elmer's face. The big bearded bear said, "I want that to be your first act in your new job. Increase the order for *The Joy of Sex*. Seventy-five for starters. We can pick up more from Book People or L-S if they move as fast as I expect them to."

"How?"

"How what?"

"How do I incuh,crease the order?" Hoop asked.

Elmer shrugged. "You just pick up the phone, and—"

"Sssss...top right there."

"Huh?"

"That's the reason I'm no guh,good for this juh,dge...ob, Elmer. I duh,don't duh,do phuh,phones."

Elmer brought his heavy eyebrows together and chewed on his lower lip. "Hmm." Then he let his eyebrows free, and they drifted up into his forehead and he said, "Try this on. We have someone else do your phoning for you. You tell her what to say, she says it. What about that? I happen to know just the person who'd be glad to help you out. She loves the phone."

"She?" Hoop asked. "You mean Beh,Bernice? She already has puh,plenty to do."

"Not Bernice. No, I was thinking of the clerk who also takes care of Cookbooks, Gardening, Kids' Books, and Eastern Thought."

"Huh? That's Lucsss...hinda. She qu,quit, remeh, member?"

Elmer grinned. "I hired her back. Yesterday. On the condition that she'd accept my apology and that she'd help you out on the phones. Now I want you to go into the next office and make that desk your own. You have a lot to learn before tomorrow night."

"Tomuh,muh,morrow night?"

"As the buyer you'll have to introduce the featured author at the book signing. What, did you forget?"

"Oh juh,dge...eezus!"

At eight o'clock the next evening, Thursday, August third, Hooperman stood behind a lectern and in front of a throng.

The big reading room was filled with rented chairs, and every chair was taken. People stood against the book-lined walls all around the room. They were the literary community of Palo Alto and the English department of Stanford University, hushed and waiting for the most famous poet ever to appear at Maxwell's Books. The celebrity herself sat to the left of the lectern, on a chair behind a six-foot-long table piled high with copies of *Soft Shouts*. She wore a stunned smile. Hoop had met her in the front of the store only minutes before, and had surprised her with his news: that he still existed, that he was the buyer for Maxwell's Books, and that he would be introducing her this evening.

"You, Frank?" she had said, her eyes wide with either fear or delight.

Hoop had nodded.

"I'm speechless," she had whispered. She was dressed in a paisley top, a suede miniskirt, and boots. Her hair was now long and straight, draped over the shoulders. "Nice beard."

They had hugged. He had kissed her cheek. And then said, "Well, shhh...owtime."

Now Hoop tapped the microphone, and the audience hushed. He looked out over the crowded room and recognized a few faces: Ken Kesey, Wallace Stegner, Joan Baez, Vince Amore, and Lawrence Holgerson. Not to mention the Maxwell's staff: Elmer was out there, and Bill Harper, Tomàs Cervantes, Abe Roth, Jeanie McBurney, and Charley David.

Hoop said, "Welcome. Thank you for coming. Please forgive me if I read this speech, because that's the only way I can get through it." He looked up from the typed script and told the audience, "When I ad lib I sssss...hound like Buh,buh,Billy Buh,Budd." He got a few soft laughs from people who knew him and also knew who Billy Budd was.

"We are truly honored by the presence of one of America's

best poets, and a person I've had the pleasure of knowing and admiring since the second grade. Jane Gillis has been published in nearly every important literary magazine in this country, from *Poetry* to *The New Yorker*. She has held grants from the Guggenheim Foundation and the National Endowment for the Arts."

Hoop looked up and surveyed the audience again. Another face in the crowd, in the very back of the room, next to the wide door that opened onto the Fiction section. She must have come in from the parking lot. He didn't have time to read the look on her face. He returned to the script.

"Ms. Gillis's first two books met with critical and popular success. *So to Speak* was short-listed for the Pulitzer Prize. Her verse play, *Loud and Clear,* ran for eight months off-Broadway. John Updike wrote of her, 'This poet is not simply good, she is *wickedly* good.' I'll second that."

Hoop looked up from his script and told the room, "That's all I wrote. It gi,gi,gives me guh,great puh,pleasure to intro-duh,duce Juh,dge...anc Gi,gi,gi,Gillis."

Janie rose from the table, stood on tiptoes to kiss Hoop's bearded cheek, and whispered, "Don't go away." She stepped behind the lectern, leaned toward the microphone, and in voice as soft as a bamboo wind chime, said, "Can you hear me?"

There was a mumbled response. She tried again. "I was afraid of that. I have a very soft voice. Especially when I'm overcome, and I'm afraid I'm quite overcome right now." She turned to Hoop and smiled. "Francis, will you help me out?"

Hoop heard the plea in her voice, and the pulse in his ears, and shuffle of feet and soft coughs throughout the room. He glanced back toward the fiction room and saw that Lucinda was still waiting in the doorway, her face still unreadable.

Janie handed him the book, which had pages marked by

index cards.

He was trapped. Conquered. He took the book and opened it to the first marker. The sestina on that page was called "You Speak to Me."

"*This* one?" he asked her.

She nodded emphatically.

Hoop took a deep, deep breath. He closed the book. He knew the poem by heart, having read it over and over, until he could read it without weeping. He opened his mouth, and out came her words, beautiful as a brook in the woods, tumbling sweetly and playfully across the room, until the last line echoed itself in the hush.

Applause erupted, and Hoop and Janie bowed together, as they had bowed together, time after time, poem after poem, reading after reading, for year after year, back then.

The applause ended so the eager audience could hear more.

She told him with her eyes: "Go on."

He went on. He opened the book and read poem after poem.

Nearly an hour later, as his voice was fading, he read the last poem in the collection, "Hush, Now." He closed the book, and once again, they bowed to applause.

Janie kissed his cheek again, then hugged him fiercely. "Don't go away," she whispered again. She sat down at the table and lifted her fountain pen for the audience, which was lining up to buy her book and have it autographed.

Hoop sidled away from the table and mingled his way through the crowd until he reached the doorway to Fiction.

She wasn't there. He swept through all the aisles in the back room, then checked the staff kitchen and Shipping and Receiving.

Gone.

JANIE AND HOOP
TAKE A WALK IN THE NIGHT

When the bookstore closed at eleven o'clock, Hooperman and Janie folded and stacked the rented chairs and said goodnight to Howard Katz, who was already curled up for the night in his cubby in the kitchen. They turned off the lights except for the spotlight on the bestsellers in the front window, then locked the front door and stood on University Avenue, holding hands. They were the last ones to leave the store, and they had said almost nothing to each other all evening long.

"Sss...hold a lot of buh,books."

"Thanks to you," she said.

"Where are you sss...taying?"

"The Cabana Hotel. Remember?" she said. "Silliest place in town."

They both laughed. They had gone to the Cabana on Janie's twenty-first birthday, had rented a room before they *were married, and had gotten drunk together in the hotel's nightclub, Nero's Nook, where the cocktail waitresses wore tall, sculpted blonde wigs and low-cut, mini-skirt togas.*

"You guh,got a cuh,car?"

"A rental. I parked behind the store. It's so good to see you, Francis. Such a surprise!" She squeezed his hand and put her head against his shoulder. "I've missed you so."

Hoop felt his body begin to quake, and he wondered if she could detect the panic in his hand. "I'll walk you to your cuh,cuh,cuh...around buh,back."

They walked hand in hand, without speaking, or at least without speaking aloud. Hoop's mind was yelling, and he hoped she couldn't hear his loud jumble of joy, of fear, of wonder and worry. When they reached the parking lot, he tried to drop her hand, but she held on tight, and when they reached her rental car, a navy blue Dodge Dart, she took his other hand too and stared up into his face. Hoop's trembling grew worse, and he saw that she was biting her lower lip, just as she had always done before, when she was trying to catch the courage to speak out loud.

"Nice cuh,car."

"You remember the room at the Cabana? That mirror on the wall, next to the bed?"

He nodded. They had laughed so hard, all drunk and horny, naked and bouncing like children on the hotel bed, then falling into a heap and smothering each other with sweaty love, with the bedside light still on and the lovers in the mirror laughing back at them and showing the world how it was done.

Janie chewed on her lip, then took a deep breath and murmured, "My room has a mirror like that." She squeezed both his hands.

He forced himself to breathe: in, out. He shook his head in a slow apology.

"Francis?"

"Warm night," he said. Right, talk about the weather. Right. "Want to tuh,take a walk?"

"Okay."

They walked together north on Bryant, to San Francisquito Creek, the border between Palo Alto and Menlo Park. There they turned right and followed Palo Alto Avenue for half an hour, until they reached the Pope Street Bridge.

Not a word until they leaned against the sandstone wall, and Hoop said, "Fi,fi,feel fami,mi,miliar?"

"We came here a lot, late at night. Remember?"

He nodded. Of course. One night they had come to the Pope Street Bridge and found that the wall had been spray-painted with a big, black FUCK YOU. He had said "Sss... omeone there is who does not love a wall," and she had called that a frosty remark, and they had laughed and kissed. That was then.

She turned around and put her elbows on the wall. He did the same, and they stared down into the creek bed, which was lit by the street lamp.

"There's almost no water down there in the creek," she said.

"It's late in the sss...hummer."

"Is it too late?" She leaned her shoulder against his arm. "For us, Francis? Too late?"

Hoop shook his head a bit and kept his eyes on the thin, slow stream below them.

"Hmm?" she asked.

"How's Robin?" he asked back.

"He's okay, I guess. We stopped seeing each other a few years ago, when I stopped needing him. Or when he stopped

needing me to need him."

"Sounds fami,mi,miliar."

"So you see, I mean, see...if only for old time's sake, or maybe for more than that, but...oh, Frankie, don't you want to come spend a night with me?"

Hoop stopped shaking. Flustered and strongly tempted, if only for old time's sake, but careful of his heart, he said, "I cuh,can't." He didn't know what exactly he couldn't do, or why he couldn't do it, but there it was. "I can't."

"Not even—"

"I have a new juh,dge...ob," he explained, even if it explained nothing.

Janie nodded and pulled her arm away from his. They stood away from the wall and faced each other. "There's someone new in your life. Of course there is. Well? Is there?"

Hoop said, "I hope sss...ho."

"Was she there tonight? At the store?"

"For a while. Shushh. She left while we were reading."

"That wasn't very nice of her."

"I know exactly why she left. I don't buh,blame her one bi,bit." I walked out on you once, too, he told her silently. If you remember.

"I would like to have met her," Janie said.

Hoop said, "You would have been surpuh,prised."

She reached up and laced her fingers through his beard and gave his face a gentle tug.

He looked down at Janie's sweet, pale face, her dark red hair, her delicate nose and lips, her blue eyes now shiny with tears in the street lamp light. He leaned down and kissed her eager mouth, and their arms wrapped around each other's bodies.

The walk back to the parking lot behind Maxwell's went

quickly, as if both of them were done trying to hold onto this visit. When at last they reached the Dart and Janie had unlocked the door, she turned to him and said, "I still think of you, Frank. Always. Do you—"

"I do."

"We had something special."

"Need."

"That's not all we had."

"We loved each other becuh,cause we nneeded each other. Shhh...ould've bi,been the other way around."

"We had more," Janie insisted. "We had poetry."

"Well, schweethot, we'll always have puh,puh,puh—"

"Poetry?"

"Paris," he said.

"You silly."

Their last kiss was as sweet and quick as the click of a couple pool balls saying goodbye as they send each other off to different pockets.

CHAPTER FIFTEEN

It was well after midnight when Hooperman climbed the stairs and walked down the long, dark hall to his one-room apartment. He turned the knob and found the door locked.

Locked? He checked his pocket and pulled out his keys. There were only two, and he identified them by feel: the store key and the key to his Volkswagen. No apartment key.

Either it was inside on the table, where he'd left it, or someone had come in, swiped the key, and locked the door on the way out.

Hoop had only two choices: spend the night in the store, or drive to the Cabana Hotel and take his chances. Not liking either of his choices, he gave the doorknob one more furious rattle.

"Keep your pants on," said a voice behind the door. "I'm coming, I'm coming."

He heard the thunk of the deadbolt. The door opened.

"Hooperman Johnson," Lucinda Baylor scolded through her smile, "if we're going to live together, you're going to have to learn to lock the door when you go out, especially at night. Come on in here."

Hoop walked into the apartment and Luce closed and locked the door behind him. "Live togeh,gether?" he said.

"That's what I said. What? You don't want to?"

"I duh,do want to!"

"Okay," she said. "But it's going to have to be my place on Easy Street. I'm too big a woman for this tiny rat hole, charming as it is."

Feeling a balloon of cheer fill his chest, he told her, "I'll gi,give my llandlord notice tomuh,morrow. We'll muh,move over the weekend. You're teh,taking a bi,big chance."

"So are you, dollbaby," she said. "You have no idea."

"Cuh,couple of high rollers."

She kissed him and began unbuttoning his shirt. "Let's roll," she said. "Want to?"

He nodded and began to fumble with her buttons, too.

"And we'll leave the pole light on this time," she added. "I want to watch your face."

He grinned. A man of few words, Hoop didn't say what he already knew she already knew about what *he* wanted to see.

They were halfway there for the third time, and the best time ever for them so far, when a cluster of explosions rocked the room and rattled the cheap china.

"Juh,dge...eesus!"

"Talk about disturbing the peace," Lucinda said. "Hey. Where you going?"

"I need to tuh,take a look."

She sighed and lifted her glistening brown body from the bed. She switched off the pole lamp and they walked together to the window. Hoop raised the shade.

"Holy *shit,*" she said.

The front window of Maxwell's Books had been smashed. The spotlight shone down on a mess of wrecked best-sellers.

"At least there's no fuh,fire this tuh,time."

"What was all that noise?"

"Chuch...erry bombs, I geh,guess."

"So what do we do now, Hoop?"

How responsible did the new buyer have to be? How much good had he and Lucinda done last time, when they ran down to meet the cops? Screw it.

"Let's go buh,back to beh,bed," he decided.

"I agree." She ran her hand down his body. "You're in no shape to make a statement to the press."

After the sirens had died down and as they were drifting toward sleep, Lucinda murmured, "Hoop, is this going to happen every time we make love?"

"Not if we muh,move to Muh,Mountain View."

"You know the biggest risk I ever took in my life?"

"Mmm?"

"Tonight," she said. "Shit. What if you hadn't come home alone?"

"I'm sss...horry you worried about that."

"I had to take the risk. What was the worst that could happen? Me getting my heart all broken, but that would have been the case anyway, whether I was here or not. Me making a scene, maybe getting tossed back in jail, but that was the least of my worries."

"You would have meh,meh,meh,muh,muh,made a sss... cene?"

"Dollbaby, those cherry bombs across the street had nothing on the noise I would have made if you'd brought that woman home with you. You would have seen and heard a screaming banshee. I'm not kidding. There would have been cops. See, I say whatever I feel, and I say it *loud.*" She crawled on top of him one last time and kissed his mouth. "You take me on, boy, and you're taking on trouble. You hear?"

"Lucinda," he answered, "you're worth it."

"You think?"

"She taught me the gipsy folk's bolee," he answered. "Kind of tornado she were. For she knifed me one night, 'cause I wished she were white, and I learned about women from her."

"Living with you, Hooperman Johnson, is going to be something else."

AUTHOR'S NOTE

During the 1960s, '70s, and '80s, I worked for a number of independent bookstores in Palo Alto, California and neighboring towns: Peninsula Books, the Stanford Bookstore, Kepler's Books and Magazines, Ploughshare Books, Printer's Inc., and Kepler's of Los Altos. I also had friends who worked for Shirley Cobb's, Books Inc., A Clean Well-Lighted Place for Books, Central Avenue Books, Guild Bookshop, Stacey's, Bell's Books, and Wessex Books; I expect there were some others. I also shopped in several other stores in the area, including Chimera Books, East-West, San Carlos Books, Mac's Smoke Shop, and a used bookstore whose name I never knew across from the laundromat at the corner of Emerson and Lytton, Palo Alto.

What I'm saying is I knew the territory and the work. I also want to say, as anybody who ever worked or shopped in any of the above stores will verify, that the bookstore in this novel, Maxwell's Books, in no way resembles any of these bookstores or any other store I've ever been in. I made it up, and I also made up, from whole cloth, all the characters (except for a few celebrity walk-ons) and events in this novel.

I also want to say that I have no beef, and never had a beef, with the Palo Alto Police Department, who always treated me with respect. If I portrayed a couple of Palo Alto cops as unpleasant people, it's only because I think there can be bad apples in any barrel, even a barrel of cops or a barrel of booksellers.

I acknowledge that the snippets of poetry quoted by Hooperman Johnson in this story were written by far better poets than I: Anonymous ("The Alphabet Song," "Twinkle, Twinkle little Star"), Thomas Moore ("Believe Me If All Those Endearing Young Charms"), Gelett Burgess ("The Goops"), A. A. Milne ("Disobedience"), Robert Louis Stevenson ("The Lamplighter"), Carl Sigman ("It's All in the Game"), John Keats ("Bright Star, Would I As Steadfast As Thou Art"), Johnny Mercer ("The Days of Wine and Roses"), Rudyard Kipling ("The Ladies"), Hal David ("Do You Know the Way to San Jose"), William Shakespeare ("Blow, Blow Thou Winter Wind"), and Robert Frost ("Mending Wall").

As always, I thank my friends and supporters: the members of my writing group, The Great Intenders; Toby Tompkins, Meredith Phillips, Janine Volkmar, and Larry Karp; Michael Moreland, for introducing me to the gentleman on the cover of the book; and most of all Susan Daniel, my partner in all I do.

—JMD

About the Author

John M. Daniel is a freelance editor and writer. He has published dozens of stories in literary magazines and is the author of fourteen published books, including four mystery novels: *Play Melancholy Baby*, *The Poet's Funeral*, *Vanity Fire*, and *Behind the Redwood Door*. He and his wife, Susan, own a small-press publishing company in Humboldt County, California, where they live with their wise cat companion, Warren.

CPSIA information can be obtained at www.ICGtesting.com
Printed in the USA
LVOW12s1632210114

370363LV00002B/293/P